Voices of Conflict;
Voices of Healing

Voices of Conflict; Voices of Healing

A Collection of Articles
By a Much-Loved
Philadelphia Inquirer Columnist

Daniel H. Gottlieb, Ph.D.

People with Disabilities Press
Stanley D. Klein, Ph.D., Series Editor

iUniverse, Inc.
San Jose New York Lincoln Shanghai

Voices of Conflict; Voices of Healing
A Collection of Articles By a Much-Loved *Philadelphia Inquirer* Columnist

Published by People With Disabilities Press, an imprint of iUniverse
Stanley D. Klein, Ph.D, Series Editor.

For information address:
iUniverse, Inc.
5220 S. 16th St., Suite 200
Lincoln, NE 68512
www.iuniverse.com

ISBN: 0-595-17483-3

Printed in the United States of America

Dedication

Twenty years ago, I had a car accident that rendered me quadriplegic. As you can imagine, this one moment changed everything. One week later, as I lay in bed trying to fathom what happened, I heard the doctor in the hall saying, "Did anyone take care of the quad in 301?" At that moment, I realized that if I didn't say something, and kept saying something, the person that once was Dan would now be just "the quad." At that moment I felt I was in great danger of losing myself.

You see trauma, like life itself, creates a story that must be told. Life is lived through stories. It's how we define ourselves, and how we experience emotional intimacy. Telling your story to a fellow human is a way of establishing your uniqueness – your identity; and having it heard and truly understood, helps you experience being part of the larger community. It helps you feel more human. If the story doesn't get told—and heard—we are at risk of losing our identity and our sense of belonging.

As I lay in bed wrestling with quadriplegia, people spoke to me differently and didn't make eye contact with me. My sense of alienation was terrifying. So, with the help of Darrell Sifford, a local columnist, I began to tell my story. Slowly I realized that my patients were doing the same thing; simply telling their story so that their lives could be more fully lived. The same was true about the people who called my radio show and wrote letters for my column, they were asking for advice but they were wishing for understanding.

The letters you will read are voices of conflict and distress. They are voices of confusion, sadness, pain and injustice. But, most of all, they are people with stories to tell. After all, we all pretty much want the same thing. We want to feel understood, we want a modicum of happiness, and we want to feel as though we belong. Since those early days in the hospital, I have devoted my life to listening to stories and telling my own.

I have many people to thank for their direct and indirect assistance in writing this book. I certainly thank all of the people in my life who have given me the opportunity to love them; because the act of loving helps us feel more connected—more alive.

I thank my daughter Debbie. Not only did she recently give birth to the best little boy in the world, she has been my trusted editor and teacher for several years. She was enormously helpful in organizing and editing this book (not to mention helping me navigate the waters of Internet publishing). I also want to thank my oldest daughter Alison. For a long time I thought I was raising *her*. But then I figured it out. I believe she was sent here to teach me about ethics, morality, and devoting one's life to one's deepest beliefs. I hope my learning has been up to her teaching.

When Darrell Sifford and I met at Thomas Jefferson hospital in February of 1980, we quickly became friends. Our friendship included a few more columns in which Darrell featured other aspects of my "story" and many long dinners with philosophical discussions. Several years later, Darrell died while on a long anticipated vacation. He was a well-respected and beloved columnist. He contributed more to the quality of my life than he could ever have known. This book is dedicated to his memory.

As you read this book, I invite you to hear these stories as I did. While reading the words, try to listen to the voice and see the face of the storyteller. See if you can listen to their hearts too, and then let the experience wash over you. If you are as lucky as I am, you will learn more about yourself through these stories.

Contents

Chapter 1...Issues of Today

Here's An Overlooked Group To Study

I've recently discovered evidence of a group that has been overlooked by the mental health community, the media, and our culture in general. These people are in such a small minority they barely have a voice. When they do speak, they are not taken seriously. You might have met them at work or on the street; when you see them, you'll know immediately who they are. For lack of a better term, I've recently been referring to them as "normal people."

Out of heartfelt commitment to my profession, I've begun a preliminary study on this group. Here are some of my findings.

Symptoms: The first symptom I noticed was that when these people agreed to help me with the study, they failed to exhibit typical self-protective behavior (i.e., "What's in it for me?"). My first findings seemed to suggest a defect in their ability to hold onto pain, resentment, or psychic injuries. For example, one of my patients is a man who grew up with an alcoholic father who left when he was young. Despite all of the rich opportunity for suffering this injury affords, he says things such as, "I guess he did the best he could. Those years were tough but I'm OK." It appears that these people are unable to feel much of the righteous indignation so many of the rest of us seem to enjoy.

Another symptom is that they appear to be happy. The world looks good to them, and they seem to enjoy their lives.

If they're in a relationship, they have a tendency to accept their partner for what he or she is and not to try to change each other. If they are not in a relationship, they seem to be relatively comfortable and, for some reason, don't spend much time hating their last partner.

From those I've studied, they tend to actually enjoy their children and don't micromanage their lives. I've also discovered that several of them actually trust their children's judgment. On occasion, many of them have demonstrated affection and even gratitude to their parents for what they have done for them.

They also seem to have a defect in their ability to blame. If they're experiencing a problem, they seem unable to blame friends, family, situations, or even themselves for it.

Work is another area where these people behave strangely. Many of them work only about 40 hours a week. They rarely bring work home or work on weekends. Most of them don't have faxes, laptops, or even e-mail. Overall, they don't worry much about work.

Speaking of worrying, I believe they have a defect in this area too. They seem unable to sustain the activity of worrying over a long period of time. Several of them looked at me and shrugged when I asked them questions about worrying.

Most of them also seem to care about their neighbors and their neighborhoods. Many actually care very deeply about people they've never even met (i.e., people in other neighborhoods, groups, or countries). They also seem to care a good deal about their world, their environment, and their children's future. They're also terribly respectful of people, trees, flowers, and animals.

Now, back to the issue of whether this syndrome is contagious. There is some preliminary evidence that it is. After spending many hours with a group of these people, I actually began to feel happy.

Groups Affected: This syndrome seems to affect all ethnic and racial groups regardless of age or economics. I have found, however, three groups who are at a much higher risk of being affected.

- Children below the age of 6 or 7. Early findings suggest that the majority of these groups are actually normal. However, most seem to outgrow it well before puberty.
- Another group at risk is older people who seem to appreciate their lives and have coped well with their losses.
- In general, I have found a high incidence of this syndrome among people who have a sense of purpose in their lives. They seem to know what is important for them to accomplish while they're on this Earth, and they're actually doing it.

Treatment: As of now there is no known cure. But rest assured, if we continue living life the way we do (not taking care of one another or our environment, blaming others for our problems, and nurturing our injures), I'm sure this group will continue to be a small minority and not threaten the rest of us.

We're All Suffering From Anxiety, But Why?

Our nation has developed an anxiety disorder. This anxiety affects the way we care for our loved ones and ourselves. It affects how we vote, shop, eat, sleep, and even how we think. Most of all, it affects how much we enjoy our lives.

I don't know about you, but almost everyone I know suffers with anxiety. Despite living in the midst of a robust economy, most people have financial anxiety. We have anxiety about our children, our future, our neighbors, and our intimate relationships.

How pervasive is this anxiety? Doctors report that the majority of visits to their offices are anxiety related. More than half of all Americans report some symptoms of a sleep disorder, and the age of first heart attacks has been getting lower over the last two decades. The incidence of depression and eating disorders continues to increase, and more symptoms of emotional disturbance are showing up in our children at younger ages. It's not unusual to see a little girl, as young as 5 or 6 years old, complain that she doesn't like her body.

Most children I speak with, as young as 10 years old, complain about too much stress in their lives. Many of these children live with parents who are striving to achieve more and, as a result, are less available and more at risk for their own stress-related illnesses. Partly as a result, drug experimentation, like sexual experimentation, now typically begins in junior high school—all in a failed pursuit of safety, security, understanding, and love.

In today's society, we try to accumulate more possessions, achieve more wealth and power, and move farther from our neighbors. We work more hours and sleep less; all in an effort to control this anxiety.

All humans ultimately want the same things: safety, security, understanding, and love. When we don't feel these things, we develop anxiety; and much of our behavior is about the pursuit of those things.

Road rage, domestic violence, work-a-holism, relentless striving for more, and racial and ethnic discrimination are all misguided efforts to pursue security, safety, understanding, or love. The effort doesn't work and could actually make the anxiety worse. That's because everything we wish for is in the context of relationships. All of the self-absorbed efforts to control anxiety by controlling our environment can make us feel more alienated and alone.

Anxiety has always been with us; and, within limits, it can save our lives. Of course, we need to know when there is a real threat to the safety and welfare of our loved ones or ourselves; and anxiety alerts us to that.

Unfortunately, most of the anxiety we suffer with today is about perceived threat. Paradoxically, this type of anxiety might be related to our robust economy. That's because anxiety and possessions go hand in hand. Probably the first anxiety disorder was shortly after the first caveman moved out of the cave and built a stone hut. Once that had become a possession, he had to worry about losing it to a real or imagined enemy.

So what did he do? Yesterday—the club; today—the semiautomatic weapon. All in an effort to diminish anxiety.

We also know that anxiety is contagious. Just take note of how your body feels the next time you are in the presence of someone who is highly anxious. In very short order, you will become tense and uncomfortable. So when our neighbor buys a gun in an effort to control his anxiety, our anxiety increases. When we are told that certain ethnic or socioeconomic groups are a threat to us, we feel anxiety and do everything we can to create distance between "us" and "them." It's too bad, because the more distance we create between others and ourselves the more anxiety we feel; all in a failed pursuit of safety, security, understanding, and love.

People with anxiety disorders often develop ritualized ways of coping with anxiety. In its most extreme forms, Obsessive-Compulsive Disorder may cause people to engage in ritualized behavior hundreds of times in an effort to control their anxiety. For example, someone who fears contamination may wash his or her hands 100 times. At first, this ritual may diminish the intensity of the anxiety; but when the ritual is no longer effective, the person simply increases the number of hand washings rather than examining the ritual.

So it is with us. If we feel financial anxiety, we try to accumulate more wealth. When that doesn't work, we try even harder. When our relentless pursuit of intimacy in a relationship fails to make us feel safe or secure, we change relationships and engage in the same relentless pursuit. As a culture, when locking up criminals for longer periods of time fails to control our fear of crime, we lock up more for longer periods of time; and the anxiety gets worse.

In an effort to control the anxiety, we strive to pursue, achieve, and protect ourselves. Yet, the real wish is for safety and love. This conflict gets played out clearly in the bookstore. Usually there is at least one large display of books about power and wealth, diet, beauty, or longevity; while another large display is usually about spirituality and serenity.

How did we get here? Nobody knows for sure, but our incredible intelligence has been both a curse and a blessing. Technology has saved millions of lives including my own, but it has also changed our expectations of ourselves. Because we can move at lightning speed, we now feel we should. The pharmaceutical industry and plastic surgeons tell us we can both look good and feel good without making much effort.

Therefore, when we have feelings that aren't good like anxiety; sadness; emptiness; or fear, we begin to think that there is something wrong with us and that we need to be fixed.

As a culture, our incredible wealth tells us we can "have it all;" and when we don't, there is a problem. Because of the speed of our world, most of us know who and what we would like to be; but few of us have the time to sit back and reflect and think about who we really are at the core.

Celebrate Independence Day

"When in the course of human events, it becomes necessary for one people to dissolve the political bands which have connected them to one another…" These opening words from the Declaration of Independence changed the world in 1776.

However, when we celebrate Independence Day, we must remember that we are a dependent nation and world. We, as a people, are not only dependent upon each other politically, but economically, socially, and psychologically as well.

For example, many people feel they are independent of street people, poor people, old people, or handicapped people. But as the number and suffering of these disenfranchised groups grow (and they are), so does the anxiety of "mainstream" society.

Companies that downsize in order to increase profits rather than take care of their employees also ignore their dependency. When people are laid off from work, anxiety in the corporation goes up, while loyalty goes down. Everything suffers, even the bottom line!

As a society, we've done a variety of things to control our anxiety. Much of what we've done depends on the political climate. Like any other family, we've tried a variety of things to help the "problem." Over the years, we've given and withdrawn money. We've pretended the problems didn't exist; and we've been concerned, fearful, and most recently, angry.

My experience, as a family therapist, is that family problems don't get better until the family accepts that the problem is the family's problem and not the problem of any one person. Blame stops at this point, and everyone can work together independently for the good of the family.

However, we have grown to hold this characteristic of independence in high esteem. Fifteen years ago, when I was initially confined to a wheelchair, my doctor told me that if I was in a motorized wheelchair, I would be more independent than I would be in a manual wheelchair. Wrong! I am as dependent on my battery-operated wheelchair as I am on whoever pushed the other chair. My dependency didn't go away; it just put on a different face.

This hidden dependency takes many forms for people. Often children who are "acting out" (failing in school, running away, etc.) are really saying to their families, "I need more of you than I've been getting. I need you to help me, to take care of me, to control me, and to make my world safe and secure." Because we value independence so much, most of us don't even know when we're needy let alone acknowledge it.

Perhaps the reason parents get so fearful or furious when their children act out is because we need them almost as much as they need us. We tell our children to be strong, not to cry, to grow up and be a "real man"—be a "big" girl or boy. Granted, I believe it's human instinct to seek independence. All children at a certain age want to be free of their diapers, training wheels, or life jackets.

To be dependent has become shameful, and we have become embarrassed about it. Therefore, we tell our loved ones and ourselves that we're independent. I recently treated a couple that had been married ten stormy years. The husband would say things like, "If you aren't more sexual with me, I'll leave you." The wife would make statements like, "If you don't spend more time with me, I don't care if you leave." A sad commentary that the culmination of this conflict could leave two people alone. However, as they worked in therapy and became more vulnerable, the husband was finally able to say, "I need you to hold me; my life is difficult, my days are long, and my nurturing is little. Because you are my best friend and my life is so difficult, I need you more than ever." His wife responded, "It's easier to nurture you when you're vulnerable than it is when you're threatening. The reason I need to spend time with you is that it feels like you're part of me. When we're not together, I feel disconnected." A classic example of how unacknowledged dependency could wind up destroying a marriage.

Over the years I've learned that we all need one another; we have no choice about that. Our only choice is whether or not we are able to acknowledge it. I need my patients and they need me. For example, a woman who had been depressed for many years recently came in for consultation. Toward the end of the session, I asked her what she really wanted from me. She responded, "I want you to give my life meaning." I told her it was quite sad that I couldn't contribute to the meaning of her life; but just by virtue of her being in the office and sharing her life with me, she helped contribute to the meaning of mine.

We need one another.

Stricken With AIDS; He Struggles To Cope

Dear Dr. Gottlieb:

I am a 36 year-old gay man in a stable four-year relationship that is an immense source of happiness for me. I have a good career in which I am respected. I have been "out" for about ten years.

While my mother and sister seem to be comfortable with my homosexuality, my father is a different story. He and I rarely talk; and when we do, he is irritable or distant. My mother tells me he is angry and embarrassed about my homosexuality, but that he still loves me.

All things considered, I thought I had a pretty good life despite the adversities of being a gay man in our culture. Six months ago, I was diagnosed with AIDS. Since the diagnosis, I've had hundreds of emotions and thoughts that I need to sort out.

For example, I don't know how to deal with work. Despite the fact that my employers like me, I know the quantity and quality of my work will be diminishing in the near future. How can I ask my employers to accept less from me and still maintain self-respect?

I also don't know how to help my family. My mother and sister have been so loving and accepting that I feel as though this diagnosis is a betrayal and that I'll lose their support. One of my biggest concerns is my relationship with my father. Is there time for us to work out our differences? Does the diagnosis of AIDS make the chances better or worse?

The biggest issue that I cannot cope with is the idea of living with a terminal illness. How do I live my life when I feel like I'm facing death every day? How can someone live without hope? Where can I go with these questions?

Richard

Dear Richard:

It's true that based on the medical knowledge we have today, you're living with a terminal illness. Please understand that although your life may be shortened, it has been only six months since you've known this terrible news. All of us have different time frames for coping with a catastrophe, but six months is brief by almost anyone's standards.

Several years ago, I spoke with a man who was near death from cancer. I asked him what it was like to be so close to death. He said; "Looking at your death is like looking in the sun; you always know it's there but, if you stare at it, it hurts."

To maintain quality in your life, you must deal with many difficult questions that most of us avoid. You, like the man with cancer, must face death. If, however, you are able to focus on the "difficult" questions, you will more likely be able to live your life than anticipate your death.

For example, think about what death means to you, and why you don't feel you're ready. Explore what your life has meant, why you believe you were placed here, and what regrets you may have. If you have six years or six months left, what do you want to do with your time? Do you have unfinished business with anyone besides your father? If you address all of these issues with honesty, you will feel more free of excess baggage and be able to live your remaining time in a more pleasurable way.

Keep in mind that a diagnosis of AIDS puts a great emotional stress on you and your loved ones. It can waste valuable energy if you pretend to be strong when you are really frightened. Many people do this in order to protect their friends or loved ones, but what they wind up doing is neglecting their feelings. This can cause serious emotional problems. It would be helpful to you and your loved ones if all of you are completely open about your emotions. Tell them when you're scared or angry. It will help people stay close when you need them most.

As far as work is concerned, I recommend the same policy. If your employers really do care about you, they may find a way to accommodate your diminished production when it occurs. My experience with vulnerability suggests that when you are open and honest with people who care about you, they become drawn in rather than driven away.

If you already have a good relationship with your boss, talk to him or her about what this diagnosis means to both of you. If you can spell out your needs and your fears about what might happen, I'm sure you can resolve most of these issues.

Hopefully your concern about self-esteem will not be relevant later. These issues get resolved as your sense of identity begins to shift. Right now, your psyche doesn't understand that you have AIDS. It sees you as a healthy man capable of peak performance. Eventually, your psyche will see you as a man with a serious illness who has diminished physical abilities. If this happens, you will find pride in what you are able to do rather than be ashamed of what you can't do. In order to get there, there are pieces of your identity and your history that must be mourned.

To learn more about some of these issues, I contacted Sandra Mack, the Director of Clinical Services at TRIS, a comprehensive mental health facility in South Jersey with a program specializing in helping people with AIDS and HIV. I asked her what people grieve about during the initial period of mourning. "A diagnosis of AIDS will mean something different to everyone who hears it," she said. "Therefore, the losses will also be somewhat different. Many people will grieve the loss of a sense of invulnerability, such as the belief that they will not get AIDS, security about the future, and (the) selves they were before the news."

Understanding that she was actually talking about a loss of self, I wondered what the process of mourning was like. Mack explained, "Grief goes back and forth through many stages: denial; bargaining with G-d, yourself, and others; anger at doctors, you for getting sick, and others for staying healthy; disorganization; depression; and acceptance. People with AIDS and their families may all go through grief in different stages or stay much longer in some. Remember, they're all dealing with their own pain over this diagnosis."

I told her about your relationship with your father and asked her thoughts about the possibilities. She suggested that healing is possible if you can expect less of one another. "In some families, AIDS creates a bridge for fathers and sons to cross over their differences and meet on things they have in common. For others, it allows them to agree to disagree. If your father cannot meet you halfway, you can heal old wounds by letting go of wanting him to be someone he's not. "

Richard, I'm sure your father is feeling terrible pain and loss. Who knows the kind of guilt or regret he might be feeling. I would guess that despite your differences, you still love each other.

Please take advantage of this tragic opportunity. Tell your father what's in your heart. Tell him about your wishes and fears. Show him that you can open up your feelings to him and still be a man. You and your father may never have the relationship you would have hoped for, but you can still have a loving one.

Most therapists would stress the importance of being completely open with one another. In many families, this may not be realistic. Sandra Mack suggested, if talking openly or listening is too painful, find professional help. This objective, neutral person can help share the burdens of your feelings. You all need a place where you can feel safe enough to discuss anything at all.

There are a variety of agencies that have been created to help people with AIDS and their families. If you have access to the Internet, search for AIDS and HIV agencies in your region. Or you can check the Blue Pages in your local phone book for non-profit agencies.

Get Out Of This Corrupt Lifestyle

Dear Dr. Gottlieb:

My name is Rocco, and I am incarcerated at Graterford Prison, and I've been coming here for some time for violating parole. I didn't report to my parole officer. My original charge was theft by receiving stolen property. I have been coming to institutions for 10 1/2 years now, and I'm tired of it. It seems I can't change my life pattern for nothing. I'm not a bad person; I'm not out continuously committing crime. I am 24 years old, and I am a kind-hearted, caring person.

It's like I'm two people in one or something. I don't understand myself. I want to work. As a matter of fact, I myself love psychology and would love to go to school for it.

I am continuously analyzing myself, in search of a way to change. I pray, I meditate, but I can't seem to figure me out. I just don't think before I act. Please help me get out of this corrupt lifestyle. I hate it. I ask you, Dan, to please write me back and tell me what I should do.

Rocco

Dear Rocco:

A 24-year old man who has been in and out of prison for almost half his life lives in two worlds; one is predictable—one isn't. The world of prison offers safety, predictability, meals, housing—and no future. The world of "freedom" promises nothing but hope.

Change can only happen when the predictable pain of yesterday and today is greater than the fear of tomorrow. That may be exactly what's happening with you and may explain why you wrote the letter now rather than any other time in your life.

Rocco, it sounds to me you're asking two questions: (1) What's the work I need to do to make these changes and (2) What resources are available to me both in prison and in the community when I'm released?

Almost every person I've known with a history of repeated criminal behavior is lonely. Most either don't have supportive families or they don't "connect" with them. Their only "friends" are people involved in what you call the "corrupt lifestyle." For you to begin to change your life, you will need lots of support from family (if you have them); a parole officer who is committed to helping you change and not just "policing" you; real friends (such as ex-offenders who have made positive changes in their lives); and a mental health professional. You need this support because you're attempting to do something you've never done before.

All of which gets us to the question of resources in the community. I contacted John Campagna, a psychologist at Graterford Prison, who explained how prisoners with emotional problems are handled on the "inside:" "Between the closings of state mental hospitals and the increased political pressure on prison professionals, every prisoner now has a complete mental health evaluation. Their needs are described in the psychological report we do, and they are routinely sent to a counselor who coordinates services."

I wondered about all of the severe problems they're dealing with (people with major mental illnesses, serious drug addictions, and various other behavioral disorders). Would Rocco get lost in the shuffle? "Certainly the people in more danger get the earliest attention. It's the same as with any other overburdened system—the squeaky wheel, etc. However, we tend to respond favorably to someone who is motivated to make positive changes in their lives."

He said that much of the specific treatment available involved the more traditional approaches such as group and individual therapy, including 12-step programs for prisoners with substance problems. Less traditional approaches play an important role in rehabilitation. Campagna said, "For example, we have over 900 volunteers coming to the prison regularly; they range from Quakers running groups, to clergymen and women helping prisoners with their religious and spiritual beliefs, to ex-offenders who are doing well who wish to offer their guidance and support."

Aware that most of the difficulties for anyone in an institution come after discharge, I wondered what was available for Rocco in the community. Campagna said, "With recent cutbacks in mental health programs, resources are limited. However, his parole officer will also coordinate services. Again, if he's aware that Rocco is motivated to make changes, he's more likely to respond to his needs." He said many people who need help are referred to a local community mental health center. The facility charges are based on one's ability to pay. In addition, many are referred to the Adult Services Division of the Office of Mental Health and Retardation that also has a listing of services.

Rocco, from what I've learned, you can't be passive or quiet about your emotional needs. In doing my research, I called nearly ten (10) agencies that might have been helpful. Most didn't return my calls, and several weren't clear about their resources and programs. In today's political climate, there is more money available to build prisons than to help keep you out of one. Therefore, you'll have to be somewhat aggressive and make sure the people you work with know what you want and need. Don't get discouraged if people don't respond quickly.

You will have to make your future emotional stability the most important thing in your life. The fact that you even wrote this letter tells me that you have some hope for the future and that you're motivated. Please be patient. The road you're taking is long and difficult. Understand that you're not alone. There are plenty of people out there who care about you and your future.

I've always believed that it takes an unusually strong man to say, "Help me." You've said those words, and I admire you for it. Best of luck.

The Different Faces Of Hatred Must Be Confronted In Order To Be Overcome

Prejudice is one form of hatred. What we have to learn is how it happens, and what we can do to prevent it. Some types are inherited—passed from one generation to another. I recently saw a man driving with his son in a car with a bumper sticker that said, "My kid can whip your honor student." This is prejudice carried from parent to child.

Prejudice also comes from injury. A teenager is physically hurt when he is beaten by a group of kids. His physical wounds become emotional injuries, and he may feel hatred toward the group of kids. This is hatred that starts in reaction to injury and fear of repeated injury. His loved ones may also hate that group of kids. Their hate could spread to the attackers' ethnic, racial, or religious groups. If none of us felt vulnerable and frightened, I believe none of us would hate. Hatred is easy to maintain and grow. We can put masks on entire cultures or ethnic groups and tell ourselves stories about those masks. For example, we've all heard that one group may be lazy, one might be cheap, and another may be criminal. Ultimately, prejudice makes us feel worse about ourselves; we often forget to look at the human beings—we react to the masks.

We also do this in our own families. Most people feel hatred for a family member at some point in their lives. If the hatred persists, what we hate is the way the family member makes us feel. Eventually, we don't know the family member anymore, just the mask.

In the 1980s movie, "Shoot the Moon," Albert Finney and Diane Keaton are going through an excruciatingly painful separation. Eventually, out of desperation, Finney loses control, locks his wife out of the house, and beats his estranged daughter with a hairbrush. She grabs a pair of scissors and points them at his neck. At that moment, father and daughter are blinded by their hatred for one another.

Then, they look into each other's eyes; and their masks break. He no longer sees an obstinate thing that makes him feel helpless, bereft, and ashamed. She no longer sees someone who represents betrayal and dishonesty. Their masks break because each escalation of violence is a choice point. She chooses to look into her father's eyes and not respond to her blind fury.

Hatred/prejudice in any form, whether passed from generation to generation; fear of vulnerability; or hatred within families is rampant. If there is incentive, hatred is treatable. If all parties have the courage to look inside and see what they are really fighting for, perhaps, then they can look into the eyes and hearts of their enemies.

In the case of ethnic prejudice, it is not a mental illness. It is a social illness. But, because this kind of prejudice has its roots in injury or family loyalty, we can use psychological knowledge and methods to better understand it.

I spoke with Donald Nathanson, a psychiatrist and author of *Shame and Pride* (Norton). He explained that prejudice is one of the nine basic emotions. "Two negative reactions to hunger are dissmell and distaste. Dissmell is a rejection before sampling and distaste is a rejection after sampling. We can see prejudice or racial hatred as a refusal to taste or sample the hated group."

I recently worked with a young couple who planned to marry. Esther was a 23-year old Jew and Khalid was a 25-year-old Muslin whose parents came from Syria. Esther's parents were horrified, "How could you do this to us? Those people want all Jews dead. They're all terrorists," her mother said. Her father threatened not to speak to her again. Both of them accused Esther of doing this out of hatred for them.

To begin to heal any injury or any hatred, the pain must have a voice. I invited Esther's family to talk about their pain and concern with her. We heard about stories they were told as children by their grandparents about how the Nazis tortured the Jews in Europe. They talked about how Esther's grandparents lived in fear, even as they migrated to Israel, only to be threatened again—this time by Arab terrorists. That fear and hatred was carried by Esther's parents. "How could we do this to our dead parents' memories; it's disloyal to them and to our culture." Esther cried as she heard how much pain and fear were in her family. She expressed her own grief and sorrow.

Once her parents felt understood, they were able to listen to Esther's story. How she fell in love with Khalid because he was kind and loving like her father. She never wanted to hurt anyone; she just wanted to have as good a family as she grew up with.

Slowly, although they still mistrust Arabs, Esther's family is more able to see Khalid for who he really is. As Nathanson would say, "They are willing to sample the individual out of respect and affection for their daughter."

Listening to Our Children

Ridgeboro Junior High School is located in Bucks County, Pennsylvania. Every day more than 700 students between the ages of 12 and 15 go through its doors. When I was recently invited to speak with nearly 200 of the older students, I jumped at the chance. At first they wanted me to talk to them about alienation and belonging, but I thought that these kids have enough adults talking to them; and it might be more productive if we listened to what they had to say. When I arrived, I was escorted into a gymnasium surrounded with mats where three classes of 60 students each would surround me. As I waited, I was expecting children to file in. That's not what I found. These were clearly young adults. Many were far more developed physically and emotionally than I expected. After a brief awkward beginning (the first question was, "What's it like to be old?"), they seemed happy to talk about what their most pressing concerns were. I listened for nearly three hours as they talked about their frustrations, concerns, and wishes. Some looked to me for answers, but most did not. They just seemed appreciative that a caring adult would listen. Their three most pressing concerns were peers, parents, and pressure.

Many of them struggled with how best to handle their emotions when they were "put down" by other kids. About half of the children said they had been on the receiving end of being made fun of by their peers. But when I asked how many had "put down" one of their fellow students, they all raised their hands. Their explanations ranged from, "I just didn't think" to "I did it to impress someone else" to "sometimes kids really do dress funny!"

When they felt ridiculed, the feelings ranged from shame to sadness to rage. One boy said, "If someone makes fun of you, the best way to deal with that is to fight them". But most agreed that if they felt good enough about themselves these "put-downs" wouldn't hurt so much. They seemed to understand that the issue is about self-esteem; kids who try to embarrass other kids are usually feeling insecure themselves.

But their main concern about peers was how unreliable even their closest friends could be. These complaints came mostly from girls. One girl said, "My best friend could be my best friend today and talk about me behind my back tomorrow." As a result, they had difficulty trusting one another and never felt quite secure in even their closest friendships. Most seemed hungry for reliable intimate relationships.

That gets us to the topic of parents. When I asked how many of them felt their parents truly understood them, only 15 percent raised their hands. Eighty-five percent of the children in that room live in homes where they feel misunderstood, many of whom felt lonely in their own homes. For example, one young man said, "Why don't my parents listen and trust my judgment when we argue about almost any subject? They automatically think they are right and I am wrong." Or a girl who said, "When I bring home a grade they don't approve of, and I tell them I'm trying my best, they never believe me. They say, 'You can do better if you try harder.' If I don't live up to their expectations, they always assume there is something wrong with me."

I also wondered about the other side of the relationship, so I asked how many of them felt they truly understood their parents; their wishes and fears and how they felt about their lives—very few raised their hands. But when I asked how many of them would like to understand their parents at that level, almost all raised their hands. The need to understand their parents was as great as their need to be understood.

Many of the children were also critical of the way their parents managed their own lives. A consistent theme was that they felt their parents were too burdened and too serious. "It's almost as though they are always trying to prove something to us," one student said. And many complained that their parents were too tense. "Why can't our parents just lighten up and enjoy us and their lives?" Which brings us to our final theme, pressure.

The students complained that the pressure is constant. At school, there is enormous pressure to perform at their best or beyond. There is also pressure from peers, parents, and teachers. Many of them have already absorbed these outside pressures and make unreasonable demands on themselves for performance and appearance.

They also brought up several other important issues including drugs and sex. One of the girls said she needed honest information about the subjects. She complained that what she gets from her parents and the media is just "scare tactics." Another girl said, "All my mother told me about sex was that if she found out that I kissed a boy, she would punish me. So now I just don't tell her when I kiss a boy." This is a particularly important issue because a variety of national polls reveal that many junior high school students begin to use drugs and become sexually active during these years.

These children are asking for their parents' time, trust, and attention. They want respect, understanding, care, and honesty. They seemed to be saying, "If you could only listen to me, you would know who I am, and then you will trust me."

If our children leave home every morning carrying our trust and admiration, it will provide the nutrients they need to grow that day. If they leave home carrying our anxiety, mistrust, and emptiness, they will grow under the shadow of our own insecurities; and we know how poorly things grow in shadows.

Granted, there are many children with special needs who require extra care and attention; but our fears and apprehensions rarely help us take better care of our children. Instead, our fears may produce children who say, "Why can't my parents hear me?"

No Easy Recipe For "Blending" A Stepfamily

Dear Dr. Gottlieb:

I am a 42 year-old man in a second marriage. When we married last year I thought I knew something about people and relationships. I had lived through a 16-year marriage that produced two boys, a divorce, and a career change.

Despite all that, now that I'm in a stepfamily, I don't understand the rules. I don't know what to do when my stepdaughter does something I disagree with. When one of my boys does something that hurts my wife, I will reprimand him; but then I'll feel terribly guilty because I understand they're in an adjustment stage, too. I get so confused about my loyalties that sometimes I just go away and let them work it out.

I love my new wife very much. I also love my boys, but sometimes it feels impossible to do both. In the midst of all this, I'm trying to develop a relationship with her 10-year old daughter who is very different in style from my family.

How do we make a "blended" family? I know we're not the Brady Bunch, but there must be some guidelines.

Bill

Dear Bill:

Only a Zen Buddhist could put two different families together and not feel a little crazy! Part of the reason for the difficulty lies in your last question. Think of the word "blended." What does it mean? When you put anything in your blender, you destroy the nature and the integrity of every item you started with. You've changed the individual components for the sake of the whole. It works well with fruits and vegetables; but when you introduce brains and personalities to the formula, things get more complicated. In a way, the natural instincts of all of you fight against blending.

Let's look at what is happening to the five human beings who live in your so-called blended family. Then we can suggest some guidelines that might be helpful to others who find themselves in similar situations.

Your sons have lost a mother and a family they assumed would be theirs for the rest of their lives. They must be hurt, frightened (regardless of their ages), and angry with their parents for betraying them. For them to "blend," they must give up their old identities and begin to trust again; trusting the very people who have betrayed them. Think about how much healing must take place for that to happen.

And your stepdaughter (oh, how I hate that word; it reminds me of the wicked stepmother in Cinderella), I don't know how long she lived alone with her mother; but the longer she did, the more of an invader you represent! It is also important to understand what kind of separation she had (or has) with her father. If the divorce was ugly, she may be protective of her mother. The reverse may also be true. Mother may be angry at and critical of her ex-husband. In that case, her daughter may be protective of her father in order to balance things. That, obviously, would make it even more difficult for her to accept you. In any case, you are violating her family, as she once knew it.

As for you and your wife, even though your marriage is good, think of the baggage you two are carrying. Divorce has a big impact on adults too; affecting your levels of confidence and trust in one another. What about the ghosts of your former mates? I hate to tell you this; but the more the anger at an ex-spouse persists, the more the divorce isn't really complete. What about things like custody arrangements, child support, alimony, and issues of loyalty conflicts? Is your relationship secure enough at this point that she can talk to you about her conflicts? Can you talk to her about yours?

I took many of your questions and mine to Dr. Marion Lindblad-Goldberg of the Philadelphia Child Guidance Center, who offered the following advice, "Relationships develop slowly. You need time alone with your stepdaughter. However, you should spend time with your boys, too. Remember, you are not the stepchild's parent. You must find another role like an older friend or uncle. It also helps to know that you and your wife chose each other. Your children did not make this choice; and, naturally, they'll always feel more loyal to their biological parent... While developing a strong, loyal relationship with your wife will initially create discomfort with your sons, continuing this primary relationship will provide the support essential to good, ongoing relationships with the boys for both you and your wife in the future."

The most important recommendation I can make is to give everyone plenty of time. Listen to them: their complaints, fears, anger—allow them to hear yours. Please don't try to "make" them blend—just allow them to.

Addressing Causes; Treatment Of Depression

According to the World Health Organization, 100 million people are depressed in the world and 300 million people; friends, relatives, or co-workers are somehow affected. Last year alone, depression cost the US economy an estimated $4 billion in treatment costs, lost wages, doctor visits, etc.

Most everyone has felt depressed at some point in their lives, but a "major depression" is qualitatively different. It robs you of your footing. You may lose your ability to concentrate; and when you make a decision, you can't trust it. The world looks monochromatic and hopeless. Sleep becomes an enemy; either it demands all of your time or it leaves you completely denying you respite. Either way, you are tired all day.

When I first saw Emily years ago, she was 22 and described her depression this way, "I feel like the bottom fell out of my life and my mind. My thoughts won't stop racing, and I sometimes get confused. I feel like I'm carrying 100-pound weights on my shoulders, and everything seems dark. I have no future and don't think I even want one. Sometimes I think I would be better off dead."

She was six months away from graduating college and looking for a job when, over a period of several months, she had more and more difficulty sleeping and eating. For the last two months, she averaged two hours of sleep a night and was barely eating at all.

Until adolescence, boys and girls are equally at risk for depression. After adolescence, women are two-to-three times more likely to get depressed. Some theories suggest biological differences to explain the discrepancy while others suggest women are more socialized to be aware of their feelings. An American Psychological Association Task Force found that women were more at risk for socioeconomic reasons. It also found many more women were depressed because of physical or sexual abuse. In addition, for married women the more children they have the greater their risk of depression.

Many people are quick to blame genetics as the cause, but it's not that simple. Genetics may put someone at a higher risk for depression, but it's rarely the sole cause. Contributing factors could be poor family relationships, unresolved mourning following a loss, chronic stress, or unexpressed or unacknowledged emotions; most commonly anger but also helplessness. Depression does tend to run in families. Sometimes it skips a generation.

When Emily was a child, she had some symptoms of depression. She was shy and withdrawn and had difficulty making friends. She said her mother would often get angry with her and insist she go out and play with her friends regardless of how she felt. When we had the whole family in, Emily's mother, Barbara, reported that when she was a little girl, her mother (Emily's grandmother) was depressed. "She always complained of headaches and would ask me to get her a cup of tea while I sat with her and listened to her tearful complaints. Then, I had to take care of my brother. I hated it. When I saw Emily begin to behave that way, I was scared that the pattern was repeating itself."

The World Health Organization says that depression is on the rise in all age groups and both sexes. Why is it getting worse? Most of us live a lifestyle that lends itself to depression. As I've said in other columns, many live lives without purpose or meaning and under enormous stress. Our expectations of ourselves and of one another are often much too high. Three out of 5 of us move every five years cutting off ties to family and community.

Most of the time, depression gets better with the right treatment. It is not a simple illness and rarely responds to simple solutions. There are wonderful new medications that are more efficient than their predecessors were and have fewer side effects. But, between our search for quick fixes and the demands of managed care to make treatment brief and inexpensive, we are at risk for stripping the humanity out of this very human problem. Not only that, 70 percent of all prescriptions for antidepressants are written by primary-care physicians who do not generally recommend psychotherapy.

Medication often helps diminish the pain, but it does not address the cause of depression. More and more evidence is showing up that demonstrates psychotherapy is at least as effective in treating depression as medication—often with longer-lasting results. An article in *Consumer Reports*, in 1995, said that 87 percent of people who had psychotherapy felt they had improved whether or not they took medication. And contrary to the restrictions of many insurance companies, the report indicated that longer treatment was more effective than short-term treatment. The professional discipline of the therapist also didn't seem to matter that much; what mattered was the quality of the relationship between patient and therapist.

When Emily started therapy, she was initially too depressed and confused to get the full benefit of psychotherapy, so I sent her to a psychiatrist (psychologists can't prescribe medications). As we got to know each other and the medication took effect, she was able to sleep and eat more regularly. Over the next several months, Emily began to feel safer in therapy and with herself.

During our work together, she improved her relationship with her mother that had always been strained. As her self-esteem improved, she gradually stopped taking the medication. The rest of our work focused on her desire to be a writer, "I've never told anyone about this because I was afraid they would think I was silly or unrealistic. I majored in business and was ready to get a job when I graduated. But, deep down, I never wanted that kind of life."

After graduating several months later, and despite her fear of her parents' criticism, she took a job as an editor in an advertising firm and is now taking writing courses at night.

Hanging Out

"Death is no enemy of life: it restores our sense of the value of living. Illness restores the sense of proportion that is lost when we take life for granted." *At the Will of the Body* by Arthur Frank

When Susan first came to see me, she was unhappy with her life. She felt her career was unrewarding, her relationship with her husband didn't feel intimate, and she was having difficulty with several of her close friends. As our work progressed and things improved, her only remaining complaint was that her life was too busy; and she didn't have time to enjoy her family.

Because her mother died of breast cancer, Susan was dutiful about getting her mammograms. As a matter of fact, she was scheduled for one before our next appointment. When she arrived, she was visibly frightened. "The gynecologist said there was a questionable area, and I needed to come back for another mammogram. He said that it was probably nothing, but this is the exact age (53) my mother was when she was diagnosed." We spent most of the session talking about the future and what this all meant to her.

When she got home, her teenage daughter was in the living room watching a movie on television. Previously, Susan probably would have ignored her and gone on to make dinner. But this time, she sat down and watched the movie with her. Because dinner never had been prepared, she insisted they all go out for pizza. After dinner they went grocery shopping and out for ice cream. She said she had a wonderful time "just hanging out."

Hanging out seems to be a lost art. Most people I speak with, when I ask how they are, they say "hanging in." In my experience, most people who are "hanging in" really should be "hanging out."

I used to be great at hanging out. As a teenager in Atlantic City, I spent many, many hours at the sub shop just hanging out (actually I think it was several years). I first realized I lost the art about ten years ago when I went to Glassboro to have my van repaired. Several of the mechanics would inevitably come over to exchange the latest jokes, catch up on our lives, or just complain about the boss's insistence on listening to country music. I remember thinking, "Come on guys, I have things to do; less talk more work." Nevertheless, they seemed happy and relaxed; I wasn't.

Frequently, this special skill gets lost in early adulthood. My 12 year-old niece could win a Nobel Prize for hanging out. But, my 25 year-old daughter recently said, "I know how to hang out, and I'm pretty good at it. I only wish I had the time to do more of it!" After too many years of not having enough time, I'm afraid she'll forget how.

It's easy to understand why so many adults feel overloaded. According to a recent study by Yankelovich Partners, a telecommunications marketing firm in Claremont, California, an average worker receives 11 messages from voice mail or answering machines a day while at work and 6.5 messages at home. But it doesn't stop there. More than four out of 10 people check their work messages when they are not working and almost that same number check their home messages from work. And, vacation doesn't necessarily provide respite. One-third of all people surveyed said they checked their work messages while on vacation.

We live in a world where most people crowd multiple tasks into each moment. I recently saw a mother in a restaurant with her young daughter. Mom was on the cell phone almost the entire meal while her daughter ate her meal without company. Watch people when they drive; many talk on cell phones while others constantly change radio stations and some do both. It is rare for someone to just read a book without television or some other form of stimulation in the background. And, we know about television. What has euphemistically been called channel surfing is really the demise of a functional attention span. And, instant electronic devices have distorted our perception of urgency. Information can get transported in a millisecond so we have grown to expect that. Therefore, everything becomes urgent. I recently called a marketing director at a local hospital. Her voice mail said: "I can't get to the phone right now, but if it's an emergency…" I still haven't figured out what a marketing emergency looks like!

Hanging out refers to doing less in each moment—not more. And, it should not be thought of as a luxury to be done when time permits. You see, hanging out can be precious.

Several years ago I had a consultation with a woman who was terminally ill. When she arrived, her husband and adult children were assisting this gaunt woman. As the session progressed, I asked her what she would miss most about this life. She thought for a minute and looked at me with soft sad eyes and a wistful smile and said, "For 35 years I would wash the dishes after dinner. When I was done with the dishes, I would say 'I'm ready Max;' my husband would come in; and we would dry the dishes together. That's what I'll miss most. Those 15 minutes a day alone with Max talking about anything or nothing." This was a woman who had traveled the world and done many memorable things. And after a lifetime, what was the most memorable? Just "hanging out" with her husband.

Preventing Children From Having Children

Of all the social issues that trigger both debate and distress, teen pregnancy is one of the most painful. It's children having children.

While politicians ponder whether or not to fund solutions, I wonder about the children. Why do adolescents risk their future by getting pregnant? Once they do, what really happens to their lives? How can the cycle be stopped?

Suzanne P. Conrad, Supervisor of Social Services at the Atlantic County Center for Pregnant and Parenting Teens, has worked with teenage parents for 15 years.

"The research has clearly demonstrated that there is a powerful relationship between child sexual abuse and exploitation and teenage pregnancy," she said. "Of the girls I've worked with, about 66 percent of them were either abused or taken advantage of sexually. As a result, many of these girls never learned about normal sexuality or even their own self worth. So when an older man says 'this is what you should do,' they're inclined to do it. As a matter of fact, many of these girls were made pregnant by men 20 years their senior."

An effective program, therefore, should include both parenting skills for female and male teenagers and treatment for child abuse. For real change to take place, though, the issue of prevention for both sexes must be addressed so that these babies don't grow up and repeat the cycle. "Prevention for both child abuse and teen pregnancy should begin with the teen's personal understanding and remediation of their own history of abuse or exploitation," Conrad explained. "Without this awareness, even the best sex education and parent effectiveness programs will be ineffective."

Such was the thinking of the creators of the school-based Youth Services Program in Long Branch, New Jersey run by the local school board. The venture counsels teens on a variety of issues and has included a program designed specifically for pregnant teenagers.

"This (program) offers one-stop shopping for the teenagers in our high school," explained Pam Zern-Coviello, the program Coordinator. In the last year alone, the program provided help for more than 600 teenagers. This is extraordinary when you realize that the program is voluntary and takes place after normal school hours. "We've been here for over eight years. The kids know us and trust us. This is a confidential service…" said Zern-Coviello.

One of the unique services the agency offers is its program for pregnant teenagers, Hand in Hand, which began in September. Its goals are to keep the girls who decide to keep their babies from dropping out of school, to help them graduate, and be good parents. Four young women are now enrolled and 10 more are expected this month. "If we don't do something, these girls and their babies are at high risk for a variety of health and psychological problems. They don't know how to care for babies and many of them never had someone to teach them how to care for themselves," Zern-Coviello said.

Both pregnant and new mothers meet in support/educational groups after school once a week for 10 weeks. Any pregnancy can add stress to one's life, but the demands of a teenage pregnancy are enormous. For the first time in their lives many of these girls need to learn how to assert themselves and navigate in what can be a pretty uncaring world.

Zern-Coviello explained that for the groups to be relevant they must also address a variety of problem-solving skills and peer support.

This is just one of the many programs in place in high schools across the nation. The difference with Hand in Hand is the follow-up care now available to the new parents. And there are plans to expand these services. In September, the agency will open a child-care center near the high school in Long Branch so that parents can have access to their babies during lunch and school breaks. In return, the mothers will be asked to contribute their time to help run the center; they may be asked to cook, supervise, and watch the children—but it's their center.

Youth Violence

Growing up in West Philadelphia, Raymond vividly remembers how much he admired his uncles, "They always had a scam. Sure, they were always getting into trouble with the law, but they brought in a lot of money and they were respected in the community. I wanted to be like that too."

So, when he was ten years old, he started to spend time with older children who were like his uncles. By the time he was 12 years old he was stealing purses. "I thought the older kids were cool like my uncles, so I did whatever they did. I didn't think much about it." Shortly thereafter, Raymond began to use and sell drugs. When he was 14, he got his first gun, "Sometimes I would hit people over the head with it and take their money. Sometimes we would get high and drive around and shoot at people."

Youth violence is not just about guns or drugs. And it's not just about alienation and parental neglect. The causes are complicated and their results, like Raymond's story, are unsettling. One noted cause is economic. We live in a world where poverty is pervasive. Research shows that higher rates of male unemployment and a depressed economy in any given community equate to a higher homicide rate.

Additionally, the availability of guns and drugs to teens are major contributing factors to violence. The vast majority of all crimes are committed under the influence of drugs or alcohol, and guns were used in three quarters of the murders that took place last year. Although the overall statistics for violent crime seem to be diminishing, the rate of violence among youth is increasing.

Adding to the contributors of teen violence is family relationships or lack thereof. The ideal family provides a child with roots and wings; a sense of safety and predictability at home and the security and courage to explore the world and form their own identity. Without wings, a child will not grow. They will tend to either conform to or rebel against their families' expectations. And, without roots, the child is unsafe and has no sense of the future. Children without roots are not able to understand the sanctity of life.

Dr. Alfred Friedman is Director of Research at the Belmont Center for Comprehensive Treatment. He has been studying youth violence for many years. He recently completed a study of nearly 200 African-American teenagers who had run into trouble with the law because of violence. Although he studied many aspects of these young men's lives, he found the statistics often pointed to the importance of family relationships, "It is my opinion that there isn't any other risk factor for violence that is more important than family history and family relationships."

Friedman also pointed out that family relationships are even more influential than peer relationships, "The type of family one grows up in will determine, to a large extent, the kind of peer relationships that will be established. And, it will also determine how a child will react to their peer situation." Friedman suggests that if a child grows in a solid, predictable environment, not only will they pick better peers, they will also react less to negative influences.

When Friedman studied these young men's families, he found that a large majority of the parents had a drug or alcohol problem and fought physically. In general, there was a good deal of conflict in these families, and the majority of the young men said that people in their families "said bad things about each other" and that their families were "not pleasant to live with."

As one might expect, many of the people studied had histories of physical and sexual abuse in the house and had run away from home.

At first glance, what our children need seems pretty simple; love, caring, consistency, and at least one good role model. They also need us to be secure and self-confident enough that, when they grow and develop in ways that differ from our expectations, we have the courage to explore that road with them rather than set up roadblocks. Our children need parents who will rejoice in the development of their own spirits.

Realistically though, it's not so easy. It's hard to be consistent and loving when you are stressed, tired, or frightened. And it's hard to be secure as a parent when no one gave you a rulebook—just a lot of expectations. But, imagine trying to do this when you also have to worry about whether you will have enough money to feed your family or if you are suffering from substance abuse or a mental illness and all of your energy is devoted to staying one step ahead of your demons. Imagine how difficult it is to be with your child and support their development when your own development has been stunted.

By far, the vast majority of violent acts are committed by males. Today's boys grow up in a culture that does not allow them alternatives to deal with feelings of frustration, confusion or vulnerability. Violence is masculine and, by and large, it is condoned. When boys are given alternatives to violence, they behave differently. Many of the social learning programs and conflict resolution programs in schools today are showing impressive success.

Change is possible.

When Raymond turned 15, he was arrested for car theft. He was sent to a disciplinary school but failed to change his behavior. Shortly thereafter he violated parole and was sent to what he describes as a "boot camp." He said, "It was hard, but they had a lot of good treatment programs. There were therapies and group meetings where we talked about how we felt and what we could do. I started to change my thinking about what was cool and what wasn't."

Raymond is currently in high school, with new peers and much better grades. He said that before his arrest, he didn't think much about his future. But now he has a dream. He said he wants to own his own construction company. He is afraid, though. He's not afraid of failing. He is afraid of the way the world will look at him, "I just wish people wouldn't judge one another for what they've done in the past. After all, people can change."

Chapter 2...Marriage

Wife's Childhood Abuse Causes Him To Suffer Too

Dear Dan,

Prior to my marriage 15 years ago, my wife told me about her secret history. From the time she was 8 years old until she was 12, she was sexually abused by her stepfather. I was nervous about this because I didn't know how it would affect her, but I knew I wanted to marry her anyway. She was a warm and caring person, and I loved her very much.

Right from the beginning, sex was a difficult issue. It was infrequent, and it only happened when I initiated. When we did have sex, she never seemed to enjoy it. But we were still able to be affectionate and show our love for one another. Over the years, sex has become more infrequent, and she's grown more distant and withdrawn. Although our marriage produced two lovely children, a girl 12 and a boy 10, it feels pretty lonely to me.

Two years ago, she went into therapy to deal with the issues from her childhood. Although she reports the therapy is going well, things have gotten worse. There has been no sex in almost two years, and now she even reacts negatively when I try to hold her when we go to sleep. Although I understand what she struggles with and I love her very much, I'm still frustrated.

I've asked her if she's talking about these issues with her therapist and if she's making progress...

I also wonder what effect all of this is having on our children...

Mike

Dear Mike:

Childhood trauma has the potential to harm many people in many generations. Although some escape the trauma with minimal scarring, some victims become perpetrators themselves. Some carry the pain in silence creating a distance from people they love in order to create distance from all of those terrible feelings inside and such may be the case with your wife.

Although I can't comment on your wife specifically, my experience is that when people first fall in love and get married, everything seems possible. Over time, as it starts to feel more like "family," old family issues get reenacted.

Another reason your wife may seem worse since she entered therapy is that therapy opens up old wounds that may have been hidden under emotional scar tissue. Although this information may be helpful, it doesn't do much to help you increase intimacy with your wife. I contacted Robert Schwartz, a psychologist in the Philadelphia area, who specializes in treating victims of childhood trauma. I asked him how we could address your needs. "Some of Mike's difficulties might come from the fact that he's feeling out of the loop. His wife and her therapist may be working very effectively on her recovery, but he still has no sense of the process. Being left in a vacuum with no understanding of how the work is being done will only increase his frustration and anxiety. Therefore, I suggest he get his wife's permission to make direct contact with the therapist. He should try to set up a three-way meeting to discuss the issues and what can be done."

Some therapists, because of their theoretical orientation, may feel it's very important to work exclusively with one person and have no contact with anyone in the system. If this is the case with your wife's therapist, Schwartz suggests that the two of you get an independent consultation with a family therapist, provided it doesn't conflict with your wife's treatment.

In order to do any of this work, both of you must make safety the first priority. Your requests for sexual intimacy may diminish her sense of safety and ultimately make things worse. For example, if your wife is always aware of what you want, then even holding her hand may be interpreted as a request for sex. Therefore, she gets more anxious and withdrawn, and you get less of the contact you need.

Schwartz says that although intercourse may be unrealistic at this stage of treatment, there's still much that can be done, "There are many therapists around the country who are using specific behavioral and cognitive techniques to help reestablish intimacy. Wendy Maltz has written *The Sex and Healing Journey* (Harper-Collins) that describes her system of treatment. Many of these techniques involve moving very, very slowly in order to keep the anxiety at a very low level and maintaining safety. Moving slowly will give both of them an enhanced opportunity for success..."

Schwartz and I had some thoughts about how much the children should know. Schwartz wanted to be sure the children were protected. "The kids don't need to know that their mother had sex with her stepfather unless there is sexual acting out in the family. What they do need to know is that the tension and distance in the family do not have to do with them. They need to understand that it's about something going inside of their Mom and that she's working on it."

Mike, it's all right for children to know their parents are having problems. When your children are informed, they will hear about their mother's trauma that will be upsetting. But, they will also see how courageous their mother is in making this commitment to her own healing. They will also see how dedicated their father is to his wife. I think these benefits will last them a lifetime.

Don't Let Your Happiness Rest On Changing Him

Dear Dr. Gottlieb:

I am a South American married to an American. After 10 years of marriage, I continue to feel empty and unable to communicate with my husband.

I have been in therapy, alone, for a year. Now I understand what I got into: A marriage to an abuser/controller. He also drinks more than usual too. My husband is a very angry person who can be difficult to be with. He used to have many friends, but they no longer call.

He has a very bad temper and will quickly express his anger no matter who he's with—friends, family, or our two young boys. He doesn't acknowledge his anger but blames others for all of his problems.

He works about 11 hours a day and although we have family dinner every night, he rushes to finish in 10 minutes referring to my food as poison. Then he demands I quickly send the children to bed so he can watch his favorite program.

The abuse started six months after we got married and became worse when I was pregnant with our first child. What I consider abusive is his chronic anger, constant demands, irritability and sarcasm. He criticizes me as often as he can. He used to do this in public but he doesn't do this anymore.

My husband is the only reason for me to stay in the United States. I hurt very much to be a battered woman with no family around. As my young children are growing, they are also getting their share of abuse.

My husband has never been to a psychologist or psychiatrist. He insists he does not need them.

I stay in the marriage because of my sense of family and my faith, which is my strength and the only thing that keeps me happy. How can I convince him that he needs professional help?

Teresa

Dear Teresa:

Your letter raises some important questions faced by many spouses, such as, how much should someone put up with? When does one cross the line from loyalty to masochism? And what about the children? Staying there subjects them to stress, unhappiness, or humiliation; but leaving the marriage would cause a great deal of pain.

And perhaps the last question you raise should be addressed first: "How do you change someone who doesn't want to change?" Anybody who has ever loved or cared for a substance abuser will tell you that there is no way to change someone who doesn't want to change. That doesn't mean you are doomed to a lifetime of unhappiness as long as you stay in this marriage. There are options.

First, it is critical that you focus primarily on your own happiness and well being whether your husband changes or not. The fact that you are seeing a therapist is a good thing. If your happiness depends on your husband changing, you are in trouble.

It sounds as if he feels burdened and resentful of his enormous responsibilities and you feel powerless. If you take more responsibility for your own happiness and welfare that alone will change the balance in your marriage. So, for now, stop trying to change him and try to see him as the man he really is and not the bully he may be acting like.

I'm sure you want to have him and your marriage back to the way it was. That's because almost all marriages go through a stage that feels like disappointment. Both spouses wake up one morning (generally on different days!) and realize the partner is not the person he or she thought. What makes or breaks a marriage is how one copes with this stage. My guess is that both you and your husband are extremely disappointed in the way your lives are going. I would guess that neither of you has talked about this.

Most people feel better when they start talking and their real issues are put on the table. The only way to learn about what is happening in someone else's heart is to ask. Ask your husband if he feels burdened or unappreciated in the family. Given the fact that you are so unhappy, I wonder if he also feels lonely. After all, his marriage is also strained and his wife and children might seem very close to each other and distant from him. Ask him if he is unhappy and how he would like his life to change. And when you ask these questions, listen with an open heart. Don't be defensive; just listen and try to understand what it's like to be him. I would imagine that your husband, like the rest of us, ultimately wishes to be understood.

Couples Must Listen To Their Inner Voices

Dear Dr. Gottlieb:

I've been married almost 19 years and my husband is growing more critical and difficult to live with. Despite the fact that I work full time and have one of our two children still at home, I work very hard to try to please him (I know this isn't politically fashionable these days, but with my background, it's part of who I am). So, I am exhausted and feel like I am failing as a wife.

I've thought of wringing his neck, but I thought I would see if you had a better idea first! By the way, I already know I'm not alone since many of my friends are having the same problem. What's going on with these guys anyway?

Jean

Dear Jean:

In a seminar I recently held for couples, we divided into two groups with men in one and women in the other. They were asked to talk about the "voice inside" and the results were fascinating.

The men almost uniformly said, "I know there's a voice in there, but I don't know how to listen to it. It's almost like I'm on automatic pilot." The women had a different reaction and said, "I can hear that voice, but don't feel entitled to do anything about it. I was always taught to be good which really means 'be quiet.'"

So, what we have is a man who doesn't know about his internal voice and a woman who can't respond to hers. Recently I worked with a couple (we'll call them Mike and Sue) with a similar issue; let's eavesdrop on a recent session to see how it plays out in real life:

Sue: "All he does anymore is complain about what I do. I can't stand it. I come home from work tired, and he criticizes everything I do. The other day I was making breakfast for the kids, and he started yelling about how many eggs I put in the omelet."

Mike: "You're not the only one who is tired. I work all day and into the evening. My bills go up, and I struggle to stay afloat. All of your mistakes are just making my difficult life even harder; I wish you would just try harder."

At this point I asked, "Mike, what you're describing sounds painful; please try to describe for Sue what is going on inside."

Mike: "What do you mean? I thought I just did that."

Dan: "You talked about what was happening outside. Your internal life, however, sounds terribly frightened and fragile. How does it feel to be you these days?"

Mike: "Dan, my job is in jeopardy. I didn't get a raise this year and money is getting tight. My mother is very ill, and I'm worried about how much longer she'll be with us. I'm also worried about how my father is holding up. I come home to a marriage that feels empty. I'm really worn thin."

Dan: "It sounds like your marriage isn't the only thing that's empty. You sound like you're pretty empty too. What do you think would bring some peace to your life?"

Mike: "I guess I would like to have a best friend; one who really loves and understands me."

Dan: "I would guess with your being so frightened about your mom, you would love to have someone take care of you during this stormy time in your life. I wonder if that's where the omelet problem fits in."

Mike: "What do you mean?"

Dan: "Just at a time when you need someone to take care of you, Sue fails at reading your mind; really your heart—and uses too many eggs. When things like that happen to me, it just makes me feel even more alone."

Mike: "Now that I'm thinking about it, when it happened I just wanted to cry."

Sue: "So, why did you holler? If you told me, I would have been better able to take care of you. I would have loved that."

Mike: "I don't always know what I feel."

Part of what gets couples stuck is a mutual dance they do. In this case, Mike's part was pretty obvious. In the following session, Sue explained that her sense of her own value was based on how she pleased others. In a way, she was overvaluing Mike and his reactions. When someone becomes too important, we tend to react more to them than to ourselves. That's when the trouble begins!

I think, however, that the most important part of the problem is how we live our lives. We are running so fast on empty that problems are inevitable. We all need time; time to reflect and think about our lives. Carl Jung said that almost all of the patients he saw who were in the second half of their lives were struggling with issues of meaning.

If Jung were right, it would be helpful if you and your husband could sit down and talk about the second half of your lives. What are your dreams, wishes, and fears? What does your life mean to you, and what is its purpose? If you take the time to explore these issues, it might open up some important avenues in your relationship. In the process, you may learn a new kind of dance.

Son Seems Worried Since His Father Left

Dear Dr. Gottlieb:

After the horrible summer I had, I think I need a family therapist! My marriage of 15 years ended in June when my husband said he couldn't "take it anymore" and left the house—never to return. With summer approaching, I didn't know what to do with myself, let alone my kids, so I sent them to camp like I usually do.

Although my 12-year-old daughter seemed to fare OK, my 10-year-old son cried almost every night and eventually was sent home. We were together almost every day, and he seemed to settle down and was able to enjoy the rest of the summer.

With school fast approaching, though, I'm concerned about him. In the past, he loved school and had lots of friends. Now he keeps making excuses about why he shouldn't go this year. He says things like; "What if my friends don't like me anymore? What if my teachers are bad or I get bad grades? What if I get sick?" I tell him that these things probably won't happen, but it doesn't seem to do any good.

Should I force him to go to school even if he's scared, or should I let him stay home for a while so that I can take care of him and his fears? I really don't want to force him to do something he doesn't want to do. After all, he's already lost one parent. I would hate for his remaining parent to become the disciplinarian. Any advice?

Concerned Mom

Dear Concerned Mom,

Years ago I watched a woman with her frightened 4 year-old son as they approached a revolving door (apparently for the first time in his life). He looked at his mother and said, "I'm scared, Mommy." She took his hand, bent down to eye level, smiled, and said, "This can be a little scary for anybody. I'll hold your hand and we'll go through it together." When we face frightening times, this is the kind of mothering we'd all like to have. She acknowledged and understood his fear and was willing to hold his hand to help him through it. Nevertheless, they still had to go through that door.

We know that your son is afraid of school. But, I don't think the questions he's asking address his real fear. The real questions are not about school but, as you suggested, they're about you. He's already learned that his family is fragile. Maybe the real question is, "Will you be there when I get out of school today? If you get upset, will you leave me like Daddy did?"

Hold his hand.

In the face of a divorce where one parent leaves, most children his age worry about their remaining parent's ability to care for them. Despite both of your fears and apprehensions, he still needs to go to school. However, don't "send" him to school, "take" him to school. Hold his hand like the mother did with the revolving door. Praise him for his independence, but let him know you're there if he needs you. Keep close to him in the beginning, meet him for lunch if you can, drop him off and pick him up from school if necessary; anything he needs from you to feel safe.

At the end of his day, spend time with him. Don't just say, "How was school?" Children his age don't do well with those open and vague questions. Ask more specific questions; such as, "What was your history quiz about?" "Did you play volleyball or softball on the playground, and what was it like?"

Most children have difficulty leaving home when it is insecure. Your son is no exception. These recommendations, however, should help make the transition easier for him.

There are many other issues, however, that seem to be affecting the family. You said in your letter that you didn't know what to do with yourself. This makes me wonder; who is holding your hand to get through "the revolving door?" Those of us who have been there know that divorce can be terrifying, confusing, and infuriating. You may be left wondering about your future, identity, self-esteem, and your role in the family. It's not a coincidence that your son may be expressing these same fears through his school anxiety.

So you see, these powerful emotions affect not only you; your children too are affected. Children can sense a parent's inner turmoil even if it's not verbalized. These unexpressed emotions can cause a good deal of harm to children if they're kept secret. All of you have powerful and intense feelings that must be talked out. It's fine for your children to hear about your fears and anxieties as long as they are not made to feel responsible for your welfare. This will also teach them how to talk about their feelings.

In addition to asking your son how he feels about the specifics of his day and how he's doing with his life, someone needs to do the same with you. You, your daughter, and your son all need a good deal of nurturing at this point in your lives. If you deprive yourself, you will have fewer resources for your children than they need.

You're right, this might be a good time to consult a family therapist; maybe you'll find some comfort and security to help you get through the "revolving door"—who knows, there may even be some gifts waiting for all of you on the other side!

Parents Must Help The Children To Minimize Impact Of Divorce

I've had enough! I've just finished reading my fourth article on the impact of divorce on children. Of course divorce is bad… of course two-parent families are ideal… of course no parent wants to injure their children. But a strange thing happens when children are involved—any threat becomes a call to arms. In this case children have become the victims and divorce the villain. And what happens? Responsible adults lash out to kill the villain and protect the victims.

There is now talk about making divorce more difficult legally and socially; perhaps re-introducing the shame and obstacles to ending marriages that existed in the 1950s. Is that what we want to do with this villain called divorce? This villain that seems to be out of control and causing injury to our children? Well, my personal villains gain power when I attempt to slay them. My experience is that they lose power when I look them in the eye and try to understand them. So lets look at this villain and try to understand it.

Most of us who have been through a divorce will admit that it's a nightmare. And what is a nightmare but a dream gone bad? The dream that dies in a divorce is one that was forged in childhood—a dream full of hope for a belonging, wholeness, and happiness. A dream that some of the pain or alienation we felt in childhood will finally go away. A dream that actually comes true when we fall in love! As long as romance lasts, we're living that dream and finally feel whole.

Think of how much pain a person must be in to "pull the trigger" on that dream, that relationship, that family. The person who decides to leave usually has suffered for many years. There has been conflict, injury, hatred, and often, extreme loneliness. It is a decision filled with guilt and fear. To gain relief from a bad relationship is to face what can be a tremendous void in one's life. To be the remaining partner is to feel betrayed, abandoned, and sometimes defective. These injuries can create deep scars in both partners.

When people first divorce, their tendency is to blame their partner for their pain. "After all," I often hear, "our family would have been happy if only he/she would have ..." They also enter a legal system that cannot handle the emotional aspects of divorce and, therefore, fuels a sense of victimization and blame.

This situation is made all the more difficult if children are involved. I have no doubt that children are injured when their parents divorce. After all, they have dreams too. They are (or should be) born to safety and predictability. Their emotional development is based, in part, on those factors being present. That is what gets shattered in divorce. They lose their dream, their safety and predictability, and often the emotional resources of both parents.

I think children can recover if their parents can help them. More often than not, the reverse is true. Children wind up with two hurt and angry parents who are not emotionally capable of parenting. When a person's heart is screaming in pain and he or she is trying to function, he or she is not able to hear someone else. The complication comes in when someone experiences a trauma; he or she needs to talk about the pain, fears, anger, and sense of betrayal. It is their attempt to understand and integrate the trauma. Sadly, though, that need is denied to many children because there is no one to listen to them.

What can be done? A wise friend of mine once said, "We must love our children more than we hate our ex." That, of course, is easier said, than done. But it can be done. Consider, for example, the work of Talia Eisenstein, a psychologist, and Alan Glass, a social worker, who run a program called "Children First" in Montgomery County, Pennsylvania that helps divorcing parents minimize the destructive impact on their children.

It is very important for divorced parents to understand the dream that was lost—for them and their children. The longer we blame our spouse or rail at the G-ds, the longer we will suffer. In my opinion, one of the saddest things that can happen to a child is to live with a parent who suffers through life. Children carry the legacy of their parents' unhappiness whether they are divorced or not.

How do we say good-bye to our dream? Sometimes a ritual helps us. Several years ago I treated a man of 23 whose parents had divorced ten years before. He was having difficulty keeping a job and thought it was related to the divorce. After several sessions, I suggested he invite his parents and sister to a session. His parents rarely spoke; they agreed to come because their son needed them.

Usually these sessions are quite lively and productive. This one, however, moved slowly. With only a few minutes left in the session, I realized these people would probably never be together like this again. I told them my thought and asked them how they wanted to say good-bye. There was an awkward silence at first. Slowly they stood and moved toward each other. All four embraced and wept for several moments. When they finished, they left the office in silence.

Even silence is a way to begin.

Wife Is Annoyed With Husband Who Can't Say "No" To Others.

Dear Dr. Gottlieb:

I would like very much to know why my husband has such a difficult time in telling people no, especially his relatives/children.

This past week I really was furious. We had made plans for the day, and he received a phone call from a family member, and said yes to their request and that changed our plans. When this happens, I feel second best because that is where my needs are put—second. He is a great guy, and I try very hard to dwell on his good qualities, but "no" does not fit into his vocabulary.

He really prides himself on his doing things for other people. My theory is that he has a low esteem and wants the world to love him. If that is so, why?

Dear Reader:

You've heard the saying, "Be careful what you ask for…" Your husband may already be saying no in his own way. Perhaps he is just saying it to you instead of others. Let's start with what seems most logical: Tell him about your frustrations and simply ask him to check with you before he changes plans. But I'm guessing you've already done that.

On the limited sample of behavior your letter provides, I would say that your husband might be what some people call a "people pleaser." That kind of personality can come from insecurity. Frequently such people have grown up in home environments that are unstable, unpredictable, or even violent.

One or both parents might have been extremely anxious, critical, or depressed. Frequently children who grow up in alcoholic or abusive families also become people pleasers. Many have reported that, as children, they felt that if they were able to make everyone happy, then they would be safe and secure. People like this have difficulty asserting themselves because they are afraid of disappointing others. In their childhood, disappointing an adult could result in a variety of frightening consequences.

The other reason they are unable to assert themselves is because many don't know what they need or feel. That's because they've spent a lifetime trying to figure out what others need and have neglected themselves. Saying "no" may feel dangerous to people who grew up in families where taking care of others is more important than taking care of themselves. And in adulthood, this kind of attitude can be deeply ingrained and difficult to change.

Of course, many other explanations are also possible. One aspect of this behavior comes from caring and generosity. But when the motive is based on anxiety or insecurity, ultimately, it's not pleasing for anyone.

Still, all of this possible insight really doesn't help you get your needs met. Which brings me to the second half of your marriage. Let's try to understand you. You are clearly frustrated and disappointed with your husband because he frequently doesn't meet your needs.

The question now is what happens to you when you get disappointed. It sounds like your disappointment quickly turns to anger. But what would happen if you could just live with disappointment for a while? My hunch is that after you turn your attention away from your husband, you might learn something about yourself.

You see, disappointment comes from expectations. The more expectations you have, the more likely you are to feel disappointed. Think about it. If you expected your husband to behave in the way he does, you would be perfectly happy. Even if your expectations are reasonable, they are still likely to lead to unhappiness. People who consider their expectations reasonable, also consider their unhappiness justified. This is a pretty shallow victory.

It is also common that when living with high expectations, people work very hard to "do the right thing" (as they define it) and expect others to behave the same way.

Understanding and knowledge often are the result of hard work. But wisdom comes when you sit quietly, live with your distress and its implications, and reflect. Eventually, we all get into trouble when we devote our time and energy staying one step ahead of our demons.

Mature Love

I once wrote a column describing a couple that were having difficulty making the transition from romantic love to mature love. I said that one of the elements in mature love is giving up the ideal. Another element of mature love I refer to as "emotional maturity." Here is a sample of the mail I received:

Dear Dan,

I often read your column in *The Philadelphia Inquirer* and appreciate the insight you impart. This particular column intrigued me with the term "emotional generosity." Try as I might, that's not always easy to live by. I suppose to me, it means unconditional love. Could you elaborate on emotional generosity in a future column?

Regards,
Barbara

Dear Barbara:

Before I talk about emotional generosity, let's talk about its opposite—emotional poverty.

When we are in a conflict with another person or unhappy with their behavior, we typically point fingers at them and judge them negatively. More often than not, we are blind to their feelings and only concerned with our own hurt and its resolution. Whenever I write an article that suggests compassion for people who have hurt us, I inevitably get angry letters that say it is the victim who is entitled to compassion not the other person. To consider injury and emotions like debits and credits is the opposite of emotional generosity.

We see emotional poverty in people who have difficulty caring about anyone or anything other than what affects them. Emotional poverty can come from depression, stress, or even physical illness. It can also be part of one's personality. Emotional poverty is lack of the necessary emotional resources to feel compassion for others.

Emotional generosity understands the motives and emotions of the person we are in conflict with. If we are with a person who is angry, withdrawn, or more critical, we are with a person who might be hurt, sad, insecure or lonely. Emotional generosity is not easy. It involves hearing the other person despite your own pain, frustration, or anger. Emotional generosity is simply understanding and caring about the other person. It does not imply that we should necessarily do anything to help the other person, nor does it imply that we should deny or minimize our own pain. In fact, we should be emotionally generous with ourselves; understand and care what we feel. Remember, emotional generosity is not about right or wrong; it is simply about deeply caring for people we are in conflict with.

Dear Dr. Gottlieb,

I just read your article on mature love. I appreciated the article very much, especially the "emotional generosity" part. However, I do have one question. The article says, "Eventually they realized that the person they were married to was not the partner of their dreams, but a good, loving person."

It sounds as if they are just settling for what they have. It is as if they realized they are disappointed that they married each other. Is that mature love?

Is accepting your disappointments the answer? If so, I can see why "almost half of all marriages end in divorce." Let me know what you think.

Thanks,
Bill

Dear Bill,

Your point is well taken, but I must disagree. We live in a world that says you can have it all; beauty, power, youth and happiness! The implication is that all we need is in the commitment, and our dreams will come true. Well, I know too many people that have become terribly unhappy in pursuit of their dreams.

Disappointment is a common occurrence throughout the life cycle. Hopefully, as we mature, we handle our disappointments differently. Or, as I was recently told, "I spent too much of my life praying to the G-d of the way things should be, and not enough time praying to the G-d of the way things are!" Part of the mature response to disappointment is in the realization that you will not be living the life of your dreams with the partner of your dreams. Instead, you are living the life you have.

Please understand that I am not encouraging people to tolerate abuse and neglect in their marriage, just not to try and change someone because they are not the person who lives inside your wishes.

A story: Two men are talking over coffee. One has been looking for a woman to spend his life with. "I have been looking for the ideal woman," he said. "First I found a woman who was bright and had a wonderful personality, but she was not pretty. So I moved on. Then I found a woman who was beautiful, but not very intelligent. So I moved on. Then I found a woman who was perfect; she was beautiful, intelligent, and had a wonderful personality," he said sadly. "Well what happened," his friend asked, "why aren't you with her?" "She left me," the man said, "because she was also looking for the perfect mate."

Expectations cause suffering; even reasonable ones.

Parents Are In Pain Because Daughter Persists In Dating Non-Jew

Dear Dr. Gottlieb:

I hope you can give my husband and me some help. Our only child is in her early 20s and is a recent college graduate. She was raised in a very Jewish household and said she was proud of her religion. Despite what she says, she's having a relationship with a young man who isn't Jewish. She sees him during the week, speaks to him every day, and sees him on weekends.

We have voiced our anguish, and I've had arguments and a very strained relationship during the several months she's been seeing him. Thus far, we haven't approved of this relationship; haven't met him; and we refuse to hear about him. We are in such pain that she would risk a relationship with us rather than stop seeing him. She even has seen the physical and emotional toll it has taken on us. We have difficulty sleeping and are depressed. We're trying to keep a relationship with her, but this is hanging over our heads. Even during a family vacation, she called him and lied to us, saying she was speaking to a girlfriend. She even said that if she told us she would stop seeing him, it would be a lie...

She calls us cretins because other parents accept their sons' and daughters' choices and don't give them a hard time.

We have been very generous with her. We've paid her tuition and, after she graduated, set her up in an apartment, gave her a generous allowance that still continues. When she was in college, we also allowed her to vacation in various exotic places. So, you see, we didn't choke her freedom. But, when we tell her to spend more time looking for work or to date Jewish men, she becomes angry. She says it's not our business and that her current relationship has nothing to do with us. Yet, she wants approval for the relationship. Although she says she loves him, she won't marry him. I'm disappointed that she can be so unloving to her parents. Can you please help us? We saw a psychologist briefly, but it didn't help because my daughter wouldn't listen.

I am of the opinion that we should not keep in contact with her daily or see her every Sunday as we have been doing. We will be there for her if she's in trouble. We told her that should she marry this fellow we would attend the ceremony. We will meet him if and when she gets engaged. She knows that she's all we have, and we don't want to lose her. Please help.

Anguished and Depressed

Dear Anguished and Depressed:

Your final paragraph offers a very dangerous threat and promise. If your daughter wants you to meet her boyfriend and maintain contact with you, all she has to do is get married.

When my daughter was 17 years old and just got her license, she sat across the table and offered this terrifying insight; "You know, Dad, you can't control me anymore." My first reaction was angry and controlling. I said things like, "As long as I pay the bills…" and other meaningless threats. But upon reflection, I realized she was right. She had her license, and many of her friends had cars. Despite my anxiety, I realized that she would date whom she wanted to; and she would make her own decisions about drugs, sex, and school. By that time, she knew my values; and she knew my fears and wishes for her. So, after hearing her declaration of independence, all I could say was; "You're right, I can't control you anymore but that means that now you are responsible for the consequences of your own decisions."

Her words turned out to be prophetic as she went through a difficult, sometimes sad and sometimes frightening, several years. And her behavior taught me that she was right. I didn't have control over this child I loved so dearly.

You keep using the word love; but this conflict doesn't sound as if it's about love—it's about loyalty and control. It sounds as if you want your daughter to be loyal to you and to Judaism. She probably wants to be loyal to her heart and her own budding sense of independence. You see, right now, neither you nor your daughter is behaving as though you love one another. Love is related to understanding, empathy, and compassion; not control and management. Often the most difficult and heroic part of true love is dealing with one's own helplessness.

My advice? I tend to follow a simple formula: Look deep inside your heart, discover the source of your pain, and label it; share it with your daughter and hope she does the same. Please tell her about your emotions and not about her behavior. It is a difficult assignment, but when it is done correctly, it can open new doors in a relationship. Tell her about your sadness, fear, and disappointment.

For example, a friend of mine recently asked me why Jews seem to get so upset with intermarriage. Although I'm not an expert on the subject, I suggested that Jews have been under threat of annihilation for more than 5000 years. They have been hated, exiled, and massacred. And, as a people, they have more or less survived every threat. But, perhaps, the most serious one is that of the skyrocketing rate of intermarriage. With each marriage, the population diminishes leaving fear about the future and guilt about betrayal of our parents and ancestors.

Your relationship with your daughter is extremely close, and I would predict that any effort at separation would be fraught with a great deal of difficulty. Please give up trying to control her; it's doomed to failure and will only jeopardize your relationship with her and may even jeopardize your health.

I don't know what Judaism means to you; but if there is a spiritual component to it, you must do more than believe in G-d. A truly devout person also has faith. If you work on your faith, perhaps her behavior will be less troubling.

Chapter 3...Our Children

Hard-Earned Wisdom, Heartfelt Wishes To Brand-New Grandson

This letter is written to my first grandchild, Samson Ewing, on the event of his birth on May 25, 2000:

Dear Sam,

As your only living grandfather, I want to welcome you into this life. Always remember that you are the product of love and passion. This type of love is one of the many treasures life has to offer. Also remember that, despite its moments of pain and darkness, life is a gift and a blessing.

Just in case fate intervenes and we can't talk when you are older, I want to share some of my hard-earned wisdom and heartfelt wishes. Your thoughts, your emotions, and your body are uniquely yours and will never again be replicated. Most of us want to be unique. As we age, many forget that, like you, we already are unique! Most of us also want to feel that we are cared about and understood. But because you are unique, nobody can ever fully understand what it is like to be you. Therefore, when people offer you advice (me included), take it with a grain of salt because no one will ever know your truth better than you.

Speaking of advice, let me tell you a little about those people you call parents. They might look and sound like they know what they are doing, but it is an act! Unfortunately, parents make things up as they go along. And if they begin to get very strict and rigid, usually it means they are feeling even more uncertain and insecure. To be happy in your family, you must understand this about your parents and be patient with them. Always remember they are trying their best, even if they say and do things that make no sense. As you grow, they will teach you about work and responsibility. But you must teach them about play. This is something children do naturally, but many grown-ups forget about the joys of play.

When it is time for you to leave the nest, you might worry about how your parents will do without you. Most kids worry about their parents when they leave, but all you can do is your best at taking care of them, and trust that somehow they will be OK without you.

One day, you will experience the bliss and sorrow of love. Love brings joy to life. It's that simple. And to love another person brings a special kind of happiness. If we are loved back, so much the better. You see, you have little control over whether you are loved by another person, but you can determine how much you love others. The more you love, the happier you will be.

And, in days to come, you will experience romantic love. You will know you are in love when everyone and everything seems perfect. Romantic love is wonderful, but it is also temporary. Enjoy it while it lasts, and remember the good parts to nourish you through the more challenging times.

Love isn't all joy, though. One day, you will lose someone or something you love, and the pain will feel unbearable. It is during these times that you need two things. You will need people who love you enough to be your companion through the dark times. There will be some who will try to offer you advice or tell you how to feel better. People do this when they feel nervous, helpless, or confused. Although their advice may sometimes be helpful, often you will find that it is not. You see, many people have difficulty understanding that kindness and understanding often help more than advice.

The other thing you will need is faith; faith you can tolerate pain and faith this moment of pain will not last forever. You will need faith that one day your broken heart will heal, and you will again feel joy.

As a man, you may get seduced by the false G-ds of money, power, and prestige. They will promise you security and happiness but will only deliver material wealth. Know that once your basic bills are paid, security and happiness come from within. They are the rewards of a life well lived. We live in a world that is suffering. It is not your responsibility to fix the world, but if you care and do your small part to diminish the suffering of living things, you will feel better about yourself and your life.

Always remember that one day your life will be over. It was only when I realized that my life could end that I began to embrace every moment—or at least try to.

Sam, I pray that you give and receive a great deal of love throughout your life and that you are aware of and grateful for your blessings. And I pray that when you wake up in the morning, you are able to see G-d's smile.

There is so much more I want to tell you—about shame, pride, envy, passion, and anger.

I want to tell you about drugs and sex—how both have good and bad sides.

And I want to take you to your first baseball game.

If we are lucky, we will have time to talk about school, friends, clothes and many of the weird things your mother did when she was a child! All that for later.

But for now, welcome to this world and welcome to my heart.

> Love,
>
> Pop

Talking About Feelings Can Be A Help To Children And Aging Parents

In one of my past columns, I talked to children of all ages about steps to effective "parent rearing." I suggested that we parents need understanding because we're insecure. We're also ashamed of being insecure and, therefore, hide these feelings. This shame and embarrassment about our insecurity affects our ability to hear our children's wishes and needs. At the end, I suggested that if we don't work out this relationship early on, if we're lucky, we'd get another chance as our parents age.

I recently spoke with Vivian Greenberg, a social worker who specializes in helping children who care for their aging parents. She's recently written a book on the subject called *Children of a Certain Age* (Lexington Books). "Many elderly parents have learned many of the lessons that life has to offer and have, therefore, blossomed with wisdom. This is a gift for both parent and child because we never outgrow our need for good parenting," she said. "But," she said, "Many others get so hobbled in their personal growth that they become difficult to be with."

Often problem parents intrude into their children's lives with uninvited advice or unreasonable demands for time and attention. They always seem to be dissatisfied with their children's efforts and try to control them with guilt. Such parents are probably angry and depressed. After all, not only are their bodies beginning to betray them, so is their culture and often their families. They are more dependent and often devalued. This means that they need more and feel they deserve less; what a horrible position to be in.

Greenberg agreed, noting that stripped of meaningful roles because of disability and cultural values, many aging parents believe that control over their children is all they have left. "Yet, control of this kind does not bring what they most desire—the affection and understanding of their children. Sure, their children may still take them to doctors' appointments; bring them meals; or balance their checkbooks, but these tasks are done through gritted teeth instead of willing spirit."

She added that all of this happens at the worst possible time of their children's lives. Their middle-aged children may have just realized something about their own mortality and, therefore, feel increased pressure. She explained that aging parents don't seem to understand this. Feeling perhaps even more insecure than they ever did, they believe their children have abandoned them.

I wondered what could be done to begin the process of healing. The good news is that it's never too late to grow up—for both generations. Greenberg said that even more than help with the doctor visits and bill paying, parents really need human warmth and contact. And adult children still need understanding from their parents.

I was reminded of a family I saw several years ago. Sixty-year old "Mary" was taking care of her 87-year old mother, "Katherine." Mary was exhausted as she tried to maintain a part-time job; manage a house; and be a good wife, mother, and daughter! When I met them, Katherine was very fragile and had to be helped to her chair by Mary. She also was depressed and complained that she was worthless around the house.

"Mary is the perfect daughter, she never complains, and always smiles," Katherine told me. "She seems to be always happy. She was always my perfect daughter. I only wish I could do something around here. I can't even make my bed or help cook a meal."

I noticed Mary's eyes roll as Katherine described her as the perfect and happy daughter. After some coaching, I asked Mary to tell her mother what she really felt. "Oh, Mom, I am not as perfect or happy as you think. You've always made those assumptions about me and that makes it difficult for me to talk to you about how I really feel about things. I don't care about making beds or cooking meals. What I really need is your love, understanding, and your ear. My life is difficult. I need to talk about it with someone who cares."

Katherine's eyes welled up when she said, "I had no idea. I'm so sorry I misunderstood you. Thank goodness there's still time to make up for it. I can't think of anything I'd rather do than listen to you tell me about your life. If you say that's valuable, then maybe I'm not so useless."

Insecurity, dependency, helplessness, frustration, anger, and resentment are not necessarily impediments to a good relationship. Hiding these feelings behind silence, guilt, or depression always creates barriers to intimacy.

Expressing those feelings, as Mary did, can allow fresh air and sunshine into a relationship. And we all know how well things grow with fresh air and sunshine.

Harsh Punishment Is Not A Wise Course When A Teen Son Is Drinking

Dear Dr. Dan:

My wife and I are concerned about our 17-year-old son. He plans to go to a nearby college next year. Throughout school, his grades have been above average, and overall he's been a good kid.

Last month, when he came home, I smelled alcohol on his breath. I confronted him, but he denied it and stormed off to bed. The next morning, his mother and I both confronted him and he again denied it. Even though he wasn't driving that night, we took away his car keys and have decided to confine him to the house for the next six weeks.

Unfortunately, I know how devastating alcoholism can be. I grew up with an alcoholic father who would come home drunk almost every night. I remember trying to find ways to stay at school or get myself invited to friends' houses so that I wouldn't have to face him. And when I did see him, he would either rant about something meaningless or he would cry. I spent most of my childhood being angry and ashamed.

I was always worried about what kind of father I would be. I knew I might not be a good father, but I swore I would always be a sober one. I also lived in fear of my child being at risk for the disease because of my father's genes. When my son walked through the door that night, it seemed that my nightmare had come true. We spent a good deal of energy ignoring my father's drinking problem. I will not repeat that with my son.

I know something must be done; I'm just not sure what it is. Please help.

Worried Father

Dear Worried Father:

Like it or not, most adolescents drink. It has been estimated that 90 percent of high school seniors drink. They do so because of peer pressure, to act older, to defy authority, or to increase self-confidence. They also drink because when they do, they find they no longer worry about all of the things they usually worry about—grades, looks, peers, etc.

In the short run, alcohol is a wonder drug. It stops depression and insecurity and makes people feel strong and confident with good self-esteem. Of course these emotions don't last and others, more unpleasant ones, take over. Most adolescents get drunk on occasion, and most of them swear they will never do it again. Then they do. That doesn't mean they're problem drinkers.

Of those who drink, 10 percent will become problem drinkers. If one of their parents is an alcoholic, they are three times more likely to develop problems with alcohol. Other children at high risk are those who drink because of depression or low self-esteem. A child who drinks to escape a life he or she doesn't like is also at more risk.

If your child has a problem with alcohol, there can be dozens of symptoms such as a dramatic change in school performance, friends, or hygiene; or rapid changes in mood. Many of these behaviors, however, can be a normal part of adolescent development whether or not they are drinking-related.

You understandably are concerned about your son. But, you may be seeing your son through the veil of your anxiety about your father. If you can get past that, try to see your son not as an alcoholic or potential alcoholic, but as a child who needs understanding and supportive parents—just as you did.

Your fear gets in the way of giving him what he needs. The harsh punishment you imposed rarely accomplishes anything. If he is having a problem with alcohol, punishment won't help; nor will it help you worry less.

Anxiety can make us more reactive and less reflective, interfering with our ability to just listen. When we are anxious, we need to do something quickly to control the anxiety. If this is the case with you, you may inadvertently be driving a wedge between you and your son just at a time when he needs you most.

If your son is willing to talk, ask him about his life—what is important to him and what he resents? Find out how he feels about his future and his friends. These issues are more important than whether he's drinking. And please do something with him that your father never did with you; open your heart to him and tell him about your childhood and the fear and insecurity you carried—and still carry. For once, you don't have to pretend to be strong and all knowledgeable. Just share your life with him, and maybe he'll share his with you.

I also recommend you go to Al-Anon, perhaps, with your son. It seems you spent much of your childhood feeling worried and out of control. Now that your son has experimented with alcohol, you are battling the same demons all over again. Al-Anon may help you focus on your own fears and insecurity rather than other people's behavior.

If the situation calls for it, there are plenty of good programs and therapists who can help your family assess whether there's a drinking problem and how to proceed.

Childhood Abuse And Emotions

Dear Dr. Gottlieb:

I need help sorting out who I am and how I feel. I was sexually abused by my father from age four through age 12. I am now 54 years old and, as odd as it sounds, I only remembered this nightmare two years ago. Despite the fact that I've been in therapy for almost two years, I still cannot get to my anger and rage; all I can feel is shame and sadness. I know there is a steel wall of anger inside of me. Will you please address the issue of anger and other blocked emotions in children who are victims of abuse?

Marilyn

Dear Marilyn,

Whenever we do a radio show on early childhood trauma, all of the phone lines light up. I can almost hear voices clamoring to tell me their stories. By the end of the show, I'm often exhausted by all the emotions I've been feeling.

As I listen, I feel shocked; furious; sad; protective; loving; and ashamed (perhaps because of my own curiosity). In fact, sometimes it seems as if I am feeling more than the callers are! The voices I hear sound almost detached, dispassionate—like the voice is not connected to an injured body.

Marilyn, when you or any child is traumatized, it causes an explosion in that child's psyche. One effect of the explosion is called dissociation. That means different parts of the person's personality are no longer associated. The shock, terror, rage, confusion, and, yes, maybe even the pleasurable parts, all go scurrying into different parts of the psychic world. It sounds awful, but it's really a very creative way of protecting yourself from re-experiencing this horror over and over.

Of course, there's a price to be paid for this kind of creative survival. As you describe in your letter, there are parts of you that you can't feel. It is a fact of our psychological lives that we constantly seek wholeness. Since we are always trying to make ourselves whole, all of those unknown and unspoken parts like your rage and other "hidden" emotions speak in their own way, through headaches; backaches; depression; sexual difficulties; or other types of compulsive behaviors. All of these symptoms may represent different voices saying, "I'm here; I want to tell you my story, too—can you listen?"

Anyone who has been traumatized in childhood has not felt safe in their environment. Therefore, in order for any healing to take place, you must be able to experience as much safety as you can. The fact that you are in therapy is a good beginning. It's important to be with a good therapist, one who is not judgmental, not in a rush to "fix you," and who is able to hear the depth and breadth of your pain and suffering.

You must also be able to go back and revisit the "child" of your past. Most professionals agree it is important to re-experience the child's feelings—the shock, rage, and fear—so that they will become less frightening. That way you will no longer be afraid of those parts of yourself.

This oftentimes-painful journey can be accomplished in a variety of ways; dreams, poetry, art (whether you're an artist or not!), journals, etc. You could write a letter to yourself with your non-dominant hand on behalf of "little Marilyn" describing her experiences. Perhaps you could write back with your dominant hand assuring your love and protection. This will enable the "two of you" to begin to know each other and take care of each other.

Remember the purpose of this work is to make your history "history" and to help you reclaim those parts that were lost back there. Please be patient, the work is neither fast nor easy.

Frank Ochberg, a well-known psychologist who specializes in Posttraumatic Stress Disorder, has written what he calls the "Survivor Psalm;" it goes like this:

I have been victimized.

I was in a fight that was not a fair fight.

I did not ask for the fight. I lost.

There is no shame in losing such fights, only in winning.

I have reached the stage of survivor and am no longer a slave of victim status.

I look back with sadness rather than hate.

I look forward with hope rather than despair.

I may never forget, but I need not constantly remember.

I am a victim.

I am a survivor.

For further reading, I recommend *Too Scared To Cry: Psychic Trauma In Childhood*, by Leonore Terr and *Victims No Longer: Men Recovering From Incest And Other Sexual Child Abuse* by Mike Lew.

Can A Child Have Too Much Self-Esteem?

Dear Dr. Gottlieb:

I teach eighth grade in a middle-class school district. More than once I've heard children say, "I don't have to listen to you. My parents pay your salary." Or, "Sorry, I didn't get around to doing my homework. Hopefully, I'll get it for you tomorrow." It seems like they are missing a little fear or respect. At the same time, whenever I go into a bookstore, I see books about raising self-esteem. It makes me wonder if it's possible for a child to have too much self-esteem.

Frustrated Teacher

Dear Frustrated:

Traditional thinking among mental health professionals is that low self-esteem contributes to many negative behaviors and that high self-esteem leads to increased well being and, therefore, higher functioning. If that's the case, it's hard to imagine that someone could have too much.

A recent article in the "Harvard Mental Health Letter" by psychologist Robyn M. Dawes suggests self-esteem may not have much to do with social behavior at all! Dawes cited studies that demonstrated that child abusers didn't have low self-esteem nor did adolescents who engaged in sexual behavior at an extremely young age. He explained "Some people with high self-esteem feel especially vulnerable when it gets threatened, and they will often take action against the threat even when it is unrealistic. Thus, teenage gang leaders, extreme ethno-centrists, and terrorists (and, history tells us, SS officers) all have higher-than-average self-esteem and may become violent when it is threatened."

The people Dawes describes, and perhaps some of the children in your classroom, are people who overvalue their power and influence; but what looks like "esteem" may well be the opposite. It may be insecurity with a mask of strength. It may also be symptomatic of what mental health professionals call a "Character Disorder;" a defect in one's psychological architecture.

This artificial esteem can be caused by a variety of things; including genetics, trauma, and extreme neglect. Sometimes children react to their own vulnerability by inventing a great deal of personal power in order to survive. The power, however, is not based on a sense of self-confidence and safety, so it's easily shattered. Several psychologists have suggested that many children who commit violent acts also fall into this category.

A variation of this artificial esteem can come from overly indulgent parents. Parents who give gifts or praise instead of time and attention could do more harm than good. For example, showering a 12 year-old boy with praise just for completing his homework may give just the opposite of its intended message. It says, "My expectations of you aren't very high; therefore, I'm happy with what you've done." Of course, praise is good and, when deserved, contributes to improved behavior. But I have always felt that giving a child unearned praise is like breast-feeding with a nondairy creamer; it looks like milk but there are no nutrients there!

True self-esteem grows with pride and mastery. Right from infancy, self-esteem comes when children are successful at potty training or learning to tie their shoes. You see the pride on their faces. An environment that is loving, respectful, and predictable can enable children to feel safe enough to explore the world in which they live. This exploration will lead to discovering new areas of competence and mastery. But, parents who are too protective or anxious deny their children this opportunity. If we do too much, or protect too much, we restrict their world.

Even adversity can be an opportunity to develop self-esteem. Several years ago I saw a 14 year-old girl whose parents had divorced a year earlier. The divorce was bitter and both parents complained about one another. The girl became depressed, and her grades suffered. But after about six months, her grades improved; and she was happier. She explained the change this way, "Finally, I realized that, at this point in my life, my parents aren't more mature than I am. If I keep expecting them to take care of me, I'm barking up the wrong tree. So, now I turn to my friends, teachers, and you when I need support. As a result, I've learned how to take care of myself." Her eyes sparkled with pride. Almost all children are resilient. Sadly, most of them don't know it. Like adults, they must learn these lessons on their own.

I have yet to find a definition of self-esteem that I'm comfortable with. So I'll offer my own:

Self-esteem is knowing in your heart that you have value. Self-esteem is not believing you have value because someone told you so. Self-esteem is understanding where you fit in the world and knowing you can and do contribute to it. Self-esteem is having the confidence to explore, grow, and change. Someone with self-esteem is emotionally wealthy and, therefore, generous with his or her compassion, understanding, and affection. Self-esteem is also being able to say, "No, I can't do that. It's just not right for me." Self-esteem is also having faith that you are loved and lovable. Self-esteem also brings with it humility and a deep respect for others.

So, to get back to your original question, a child can have too much indulgence, protection, or power. But can a child have too much love or self-esteem? I don't think so.

What looks like self-esteem may well be insecurity. You may want to treat these children as you would any other insecure child. Reassure them, help them to get the task done, understand they're having difficulty; but under no circumstances is it helpful to lower your expectations.

Communication; Key When Child Flirts With Drugs

Dear Dr. Gottlieb:

My 17-year-old son has recently been caught getting high with pot and alcohol on weekends. Unfortunately, this has been going on for several months. I have tried talking to him and warning him of the dangers. Not knowing which way to turn, I contacted his school for help. He was seen by an "assessment counselor" who recommended weekly meetings and a review of his grades and behavior.

I am very concerned because his dad is an alcoholic, and there is a strong family background of abusive drinking. My son does not like to be compared to any of those persons, so he was offered a challenge by the counselor—to just say no if he is going to be around his peers who are partaking in this activity.

At the time, the main concern of the counselor was to watch his habit to make sure it doesn't become a dependency. I feel if he is already doing this on a weekly basis it already is a dependency.

When I inquired as to what I can do to help him, I was told to just keep the lines of communication open between us. I feel as though I should be doing something more. I have not punished him for his actions. The counselor suggested instead we use the reward system, to offer him something for staying straight. I guess I don't have much of a problem with this, but I am certainly not comfortable with just taking him on his word.

Dear Reader:

Keeping lines of communication open sounds passive, but it is difficult to do and could save your son. After all, almost any problem can be resolved if it gets talked about. But when we hide issues, they tend to fester and grow.

Clearly, he has betrayed your trust. That's why you're uncomfortable taking him on his word. This is not necessarily a devious kid. If he is a substance abuser, dishonesty is one of the symptoms.

Not only do you mistrust him, but it also seems that he doesn't trust you either. If he did, he would come to you and say that he has a problem. That doesn't necessarily mean you're doing anything wrong. It may be that he is too ashamed or uncomfortable with himself to talk to you.

Let's think about what is needed in your family to make things safe enough to open communication. Despite your understandable anxiety, he must be listened to before he is told the dangers of drugs and alcohol. I'm sure he already knows them anyway. See if you can help him talk about his life.

For example, see if he will talk about what it is like to be near the end of high school. Ask him if he feels himself changing from a boy to a man; and if he does, does that feel good or bad? I would also wonder if he feels like he fits in with the other kids; and if not, is that painful?

The specific questions aren't that important. But it is important that you talk to him about his life and not just his behavior around substance abuse. It's also very important for you not to judge or lecture him. If you do, he will close up quickly. Wouldn't you?

The other problem is that parents often lecture kids about the dangers of substance abuse, but they fail to tell the whole story. Then, the child will get high one night and feel wonderful. Once that happens, everything their parents have told them seems invalid because they were never told the whole story. I believe children should be told how and why drugs are dangerous. I also believe they should be told that sometimes when children get high, it feels wonderful and sometimes it feels awful and scary. Sometimes it even feels like all of your problems go away for a brief period of time. But when they're no longer high, the problems come back and everything feels a little worse.

I am also hearing other changes that must be addressed. You said your husband had a history of alcoholism. I don't know if he ever received treatment or if there is continuing baggage from his history. But substance abuse is a family problem and not just an individual one. Therefore, I strongly recommend all of you see a family therapist. Family therapy can also help get the focus off one person and his behavior. This can diminish a lot of the pressure that may be on him.

If, in fact, he is a substance abuser, please remember that this is a serious disease that needs treatment. You and your son also have to understand that, ultimately, his life is in his hands. You can open communication and set limits, but you can never control whether or not he uses drugs. Until everyone in the family understands that, it is unlikely that anything will change. A 12-step program could help everyone in the family get to that point and beyond. These programs plus family therapy are very compatible and tend to work well together.

All of these things are terribly difficult to do. If you do them, however, your son has a better chance at his future.

Parents Need To Know Signs Of Emotional Disorders In Children

Mental illness. Mental disorder. Emotional distress. Any way we label it, the subject causes anxiety. Despite our enlightenment, there's still a great deal of shame and fear attached to emotional disorders. So, when our children begin to have symptoms, we say things like, "It's only temporary;" "You'll get over it;" or "It's just a stage." Sometimes we suggest that they are acting inappropriately just because they want attention. According to the Center for Mental Health Services, a Division of the U.S. Department of Health and Human Services, parents who make such statements are right 80 percent of the time because four out of five children grow up without any serious emotional difficulties.

Still, one in 5 children has a behavioral or mental health problem and, at least, one in twenty has a serious emotional disturbance. That's something like three million children. And, because of the lingering stigma, children, generally, don't talk about emotions that may scare or embarrass them. They are unlikely to be open with teachers, parents, or even their peers. They may spend months, even years, trying to deny or minimize their suffering. That's why the Center recently launched a major new initiative, "Caring for Every Child's Mental Health," to raise awareness of signs of emotional disorders and to help families get the services they need.

Low self-esteem or low self-worth can lead to depression, anxiety, and many other disorders. Parents should be on alert if their children:

- Seem sad or tearful for six months or more and can't explain why.
- Give indications they don't like themselves or their bodies.
- Seem more worried or guilt-ridden than other children.
- Cry or overreact to things that seem minor.
- Have many fears or phobias, or become terrified easily.

These symptoms don't automatically mean something's wrong; they signal a potential problem. Sometimes spending more time and listening to your children's concerns can go a long way. Often, parents will tell children that everything will be okay or that their fears and concerns are irrational. Children tend to find more reassurance from a parent's time and interest than from words.

Sometimes, however, these symptoms could be early signs of an anxiety disorder, depression, or an eating disorder. These symptoms may also be precursors of substance abuse. That's because children (and adults) sometime abuse drugs or alcohol in an attempt to control difficult emotions.

Some other signs to look for include:

• Radical and persistent change in behavior.
• Change in friends, grades, and/or eating or sleeping patterns.
• Talk as though life is too difficult to manage.
• Talk of suicide.
• Have difficulty concentrating or performing tasks.
• Worry excessively about hurting other people's feelings or "doing the wrong thing."
• Needing to be excessively clean or organized.

Although these symptoms could be precursors of a variety of disorders ranging from Depression to Learning Disability to Obsessive-compulsive Disorder, all are signs of a child in distress.

Even though it's impossible to pinpoint the exact causes of these disorders, we are learning more about some of the factors that put children at risk. We know that genetics and biochemical changes play a major role in many of the learning disorders. We also know that children who are exposed to violence; unstable homes; and physical, sexual, or emotional trauma also are at higher risk for later emotional problems. Early death of loved ones, inconsistent discipline, and corporal punishment are other risk factors.

There's much that can be done to help children with serious emotional problems. In milder cases, sometimes short-term supportive treatment is all that is needed. Many disorders are responsive to psychotherapy. Medication, although usually not a first choice with children, is being improved almost daily. Depending on the disorder, drugs are becoming more effective with fewer side effects. There have also been new types of therapies developed for specific syndromes such as Phobias, Anxiety Disorders, and many of the Obsessive-compulsive Disorders and Learning Disabilities.

Family therapy is often the treatment of choice when symptoms indicate there are underlying problems in the family. For severe emotional disorders, more aggressive intervention might be needed. Ideally, a child with a major mental illness requires a caseworker to coordinate treatment with schools, social services, and the family.

Although mental illness cannot be prevented, there are many things we can do to improve our children's emotional health:

- Provide a safe and predictable home.
- Make sure the love we feel for our children is demonstrated through a generous offering of our time, attention, respect, and trust.
- Children need to express their feelings, the whole range of them, even if they are uncomfortable for us. Don't try to suppress or alter their feelings; only their behavior. Help teach your children that negative emotions such as anger are uncomfortable but that everyone feels them. The goal is to learn to express these emotions appropriately.
- Most of all, children need to be heard. I believe our most important function is to help them find their voice, identify their strengths, and give them dignity. We do that by listening, by questioning, and by loving.

For more information, or to find the proper assistance, contact The Center for Mental Health Services at 800-789-2647 or on-line at www.mentalhealth.org

Can A 15-Year Old And An 11 Year-Old Be Friends?

I recently received the following e-mails from a worried young man.

Dear Dr. Dan:

We live in Philadelphia, and I have lived here for 15 years. Now my mother wants to move 2 ½ hours away. I have this one particular friend who is only 11 years old but I love him like a little brother. I am 15. Is there something wrong with hangin' with an 11-year old? We might not be moving, and I pray to G-d we don't for I will be heart-broken, and I don't know if I can live like that. Can you help?

Dear Reader:

First of all, there is not necessarily anything wrong with your having a good friend who is four years younger than you. It's possible that neither of you have brothers, or good relationships with brothers, and have found that kind of companionship in each other. It's also possible that one or both of you may feel like you don't "fit" well with your classmates. The third possibility is that you just really like each other!

If your mother does move, I'm sure the loss will be very painful and sad. Perhaps you and your friend could find a way to meet every now and then or, at the very least, exchange letters, or e-mail. Try to make it clear to your mother how sad and painful this situation is. If she understands, she might help you find a way to keep in touch with him.

Dear Dr. Dan:

Thanks a lot for the letter. The thing is, I can't really talk to my mom about this because she does not take my feelings seriously. She thinks it is ridiculous to feel that way about an 11-year old you barely know. I have known him for 13 months. I mean, he is a good kid; very smart and he tells me I am his best friend. We talk to each other in school, he tells me he will miss me, and doesn't want me to leave. Now I know young kids can be using me. I am older and stuff. But he has proved to me that he is not.

Dear Reader:

Many people your age complain that their parents don't hear them. It's sad because I think a parent's most important job is listening to their children. Several years ago, I was treating a young woman who was going through a crisis. I asked her if her mother could be helpful—supportive. She said, "No, my mother can't hear my heart." That sounds like what you are saying—your mother can't hear your heart. Usually, when adults aren't able to listen to their children, the adults are either distressed or emotionally depleted. And often they feel isolated and alone.

Your mother might feel she has no choice about moving, and she may be feeling very stressed and isolated just as you do. It's too bad that you guys can't seem to talk about it. Because I would think that if she could just understand how sad you are, it might make it a little better for you; and if you could understand what things were like for her, she might also feel better.

In any event, here is a poem about friendship by Langston Hughes that you might want to share with your friend:

> I loved my friend.
> He went away from me.
> There's nothing more to say.
> The poem ends, soft as it began—
> I loved my friend.

Most acts of violence are committed by boys; boys who are unable to handle their vulnerable feelings—sadness, dependency, feeling out of control, fear, and many others. Boys are socialized to be strong, and most are taught that these vulnerable feelings are either shameful or unmanly. When our sons feel sad or frightened, we need to embrace them and listen. The alternative could be awful.

A Distressed Daughter, 12, Needs To Feel Safe

Dear Dr. Gottlieb:

My daughter is 12 years old and having a terrible time dealing with her peers. She can be very insulting, condescending, and even mean. It was her biggest problem in school last year, and she had similar conflicts in camp this summer. I suggested counseling in the past, but she doesn't admit to having a problem. She feels she is always the victim.

I am at a loss. I've taken a look at myself to see if I possess these qualities, and I've even asked my friends; but they say I don't. I'm willing to go for help if that would help her. It's as though there is something missing from my daughter.

Linda
P.S. Her father lives several hundred miles away; and even though she sees him once a month and talks to him on the phone, he has not been an active part of her life for many years.

Dear Linda,

Let's try to read the language of your daughter's behavior. It seems to be saying, "My surroundings feel uncomfortable. In addition, I am powerless because I feel like a victim. No matter where I go, I don't seem to fit." Of course I am just guessing about what's happening with her, but we do know she is feeling a good deal of distress.

Part of the problem might be her age. Early adolescence can be a very difficult time for girls. This is a time when girls often have diminished self-esteem and increased anxiety. Frequently, they are more irritable and self-conscious. Their relationships with boys frequently change and can shift from friends and equals one day to something that feels sexualized and out of balance the next. Relationships with girlfriends can also turn extremely competitive and shame-based. This stage of life can be pretty lonely and confusing.

Emotions that might have been lying dormant can manifest themselves during this time. Which brings us to the issue of her father. Some girls don't experience significant distress about a father's absence until puberty. As a girl develops into a woman, she needs her father more than ever. A father's role is to help girls feel attractive, competent, and lovable. Often a father's image of his daughter contributes significantly to her image of herself. Many women I've treated who have lost fathers through divorce or death feel unattractive, not bright, or guilty about being sexual. A girl can really blossom when she experiences her father's pride and affection as she enters womanhood.

So here she is, on the brink of womanhood, not feeling comfortable with herself or her environment. We know she's had little guidance from her father, but we don't know what she has or hasn't learned from you.

My experience in working with people like your daughter is that confrontation rarely helps. People usually don't express or acknowledge their more vulnerable feelings because they don't feel safe enough to do so. Understanding brings safety.

A middle-aged woman I work with had a difficult relationship with her mother during her adolescence. She described her mother as rigid, demanding, and unavailable. Her parents divorced when she was seven, and she rarely saw her father. My patient felt abandoned, angry, and frightened. But, she was unable to express these feelings. Nearly 30 years later, she still suffered from insecurity and hidden resentment. So, I invited her to bring her mother to a session.

When they arrived, their anxiety filled the room. Nevertheless, I invited the mother to talk about her life. She told us about her experience of what it was like to be a woman in the 1950s; how oppressed and powerless she felt. She talked about her relationship with her own mother who, she claimed, never had time to offer her guidance when she desperately needed it. And she talked about how she tried to raise her own daughter to be "perfect" in her failed attempt to finally make her own mother proud.

She cried as she talked about her grief and regret and her lonely struggle to discover her own womanhood. As my client moved her hand over to hold her mother's, she said, "If I had known this about you when I was 15, everything would have been different. These are many of the same emotions I feel today. Now I don't feel alone."

Although I don't think the symptoms your daughter is showing portend anything catastrophic, you are right to seek help. My hunch is she has many feelings that need to be expressed, but she doesn't know how. The same may be the case with you. Remember, through your actions you are teaching her about being a woman. If you open your heart to her, it will make her world more open and honest and, therefore, safer. And, if you're able to be open with her, eventually she'll be open with you.

Don't hesitate to tell her your dreams, fears, and disappointments. Most of all, tell her what it's like to be a woman; the good news and the bad news. If you treat her like a trusted family member, she will have found a least one environment in which she feels comfortable.

Don't give up on therapy, especially family therapy. But when you go, remember that she is not the patient. After all, both of you are in pain.

Girl's "Best Friends" Suddenly Pick On Her In Middle School

Dear Dan Gottlieb:

I am concerned about a problem my daughter is having in middle school. Her "best friends" from last year's fifth grade have intentionally alienated her from this group, starting with the first day of school. These girls have not given her any reason for this behavior.

They are also very mean to my daughter. They won't speak to her, they push her in the halls, and they have been pushing books out of her hands.

They have enlisted other girls to treat her the same way. They call her a loser.

We have encouraged our daughter to make new friends which hasn't been easy since this group of girls seems to wield much power in the school. I have noticed my once very self-confident child losing a great deal of self-esteem. It has also been very stressful in our household the last few months. Any suggestions?

Concerned Mother

Dear Mother:

It seems that children have forever been picking on one another. Today, though, the activity seems more mean-spirited. Sadly, our children live in a world where they see many adults doing the same thing. We criticize our neighbors, complain about friends or family members, and pass judgment on other groups. I believe that children who live in a family that practices acceptance and compassion for others will be unlikely to hurt their peers in school.

There is another factor at play here. Very likely, your daughter and her peers are in the early stages of puberty. A good deal of research suggests girls at this stage of life have greatly diminished self-esteem. And we know one of the ways children cope with diminished self-esteem is to find some-one to "put down." Add to this mix the fact that middle school is frequently when kids are introduced to drugs and sex. This situation puts children at risk for insecurity, identity problems, competitiveness, and alienation.

Even though most children report that their peers at one point in their lives have ostracized them, the emotional pain that accompanies this alienation can go beyond temporary hurt and anger to diminished self-esteem. It can also contribute to withdrawal, poor academic performance, and even depression. And sadly, we all know that in its most extreme form, alienation can contribute to hopelessness and violence.

Let's talk about what can be done for your daughter. First, it is important that you ask her what she wants you to do. Perhaps, all she wants is a sympathetic ear; someone who understands her pain and who cares. Perhaps, she wants you to be more aggressive and to intervene on her behalf. But, if you let her decide, she will feel more respected; something she is missing in school. Whatever you do, please just listen before you do anything. If you get too upset, if you react too quickly, your daughter might minimize what she feels in order to protect you. If that happens, then she will feel alienated both at school and at home.

Speaking of home, at the end of your letter you said that things have been stressful at home also. You didn't mention what the stress was. I'm sure you understand that children are like sponges in the family and can absorb stress whether it gets talked about or not. I recently saw a family in which the 9 year-old daughter was showing symptoms of depression. It turns out that her paternal grandmother, who lives on the West Coast, was recently diagnosed with cancer. The girl barely knew her grandmother, but said she "knew" her father was terribly upset even though he never said anything about it.

Of course, she was right. Whatever the stress in your family is, it is possible that your daughter already felt distressed and alienated before she even started school. If the stress in your family hasn't been resolved by now, I would recommend family therapy. Whatever the issue is, if you all talk about it together, everyone might feel closer.

If your daughter is agreeable, group therapy with girls her own age could be helpful. Without having more information, my instinct is that group will be more helpful than individual therapy because it will give her the opportunity to form new relationships in the group; and she could get more valid feedback from her peers.

One more thing—I see this as a teaching opportunity for the whole school. I would contact the Principal and the Counseling Department and urge them to create a training program for the students. Of course, this wouldn't be about your daughter. It would be a chance for the students to learn about diversity and compassion.

I assume that the girls who have been mean to your daughter don't feel very good about themselves. Therefore, the training could give all of the children an opportunity to talk about the stresses in their lives. I have found that when these young children are able to talk about their insecurities, they feel less pressure to put on an act; and they feel better about themselves and one another.

Mother Grieves As Her "Babies" Prepare To Move On

Dear Dr. Gottlieb:

My children are now 15 and 18, and I love them dearly. However, I have worked so hard at being a good mother for such a long time, I never realized how much their growing up and away would affect me. I have a great job and a wonderful husband. I never expected to feel such sadness at a process that everyone tells me is just a natural part of life. Is there something wrong with the way I am feeling?

Sad Mom

Dear Sad Mom:

Over the years, I have received many letters from women in your position. You didn't state your age, but the message many women in their 40s and older have received is happiness and fulfillment come from being a good wife and mother. If you complete these tasks well, you will reap the benefits. Most of the women who write the letters wonder; okay, I did my job—now everyone is leaving. My kids have moved out, my husband seems terribly happy at work, and I'm left without a sense of meaning. So where are the benefits? I feel alone and deceived.

You're right; the fact that your children are growing up and preparing to leave is a natural part of life—so is sadness. I would guess that you not only love these children but have probably loved being their mother also. If that's the case, how could you feel anything other than sadness?

You may be wondering if this pain could have been avoided; perhaps to a certain extent. For example, if your job demanded a great deal of attention and energy; or if you had many outside activities, your children may have been less in the focus of your psychological lens. Had you done that, the pain may have been less. But would you have wanted that? Remember, the deeper the love, the greater the pain. I'm sure you'll agree that the benefits far outweigh the pain.

Of course, the next logical question is what can be done for you. Sometimes a child's departure can mean a loss of identity. Many women identify themselves primarily as wives or mothers. When these roles are lost or changed, many women wonder; who am I now?

Think about what you want your life to look like in a few years. What are the many things you've deprived yourself of to be a good mother? This might be the first time in your life that your needs and desires can take priority. The process can be confusing, sometimes scary, and often exhilarating. It also may be helpful to speak with other women in your position.

By the way, there is a good deal of research that suggests the so-called empty-nest women actually find a new lease on life after the children leave. Many women report that they feel more energy and a greater sense of freedom. And now that the children are no longer home and many of the women are past menopause, they report enjoying their sexuality more than ever before. And keep in mind that if your sadness gets worse, it could be the early stages of depression. If you find changes in your sleep patterns, appetite, sexual interest, or work performance, contact a mental health professional. Depression is very treatable.

Remember, though, that sadness is not an illness—just a reaction to loss.

* * *

Children Need Patience With Their Insecure, Embarrassed Parents

During a family session last month, an angry 10 year-old boy said to me, "I think when babies are born a machine comes out of the sky, attaches itself to the parents' heads, and sucks something out of their brain!"

I was shocked when I heard this. After all, we parents are sworn to secrecy. How did he find out? I confronted his parents, "Did you tell him our secret?" "No," they asserted (they looked honest, but I'm still not sure I believe them). Anyway, now that the secret's out, I might as well tell the whole truth. If you're a parent, I urge you to not read further; this column may be too revealing. It's really only designed for children of all ages.

There are several points to effective parent rearing that children should know:

- Something was, in fact, sucked out of your parents' brains when you were born. I'm not quite sure what it was (after all, I am a parent, too, and suffered the same fate); but if you want to be a good parent manager, you have to understand that the people you're raising have this defect. Therefore, we should be treated carefully, with understanding, and compassion. If you were raising someone else with a defect, you would have a good deal of tolerance for them—why not us?

- We are all insecure. Being told we are responsible for a baby without giving us a good rulebook, will make anyone insecure (but to add to our problems, we've had that "stuff" sucked out of our brains, so that we're working with fewer tools). We're also told by our parents (and society) that we must raise our children to be almost perfect or else we're not good enough. If they wind up distressed or in pain, we have to spend thousands of dollars for their therapy in which we get blamed for their problems. This is a very frightening prospect for parents, but we're too insecure to admit it. So parents need to be treated as you would treat anyone else who is frightened and insecure.

- We hide our insecurity. We are ashamed and embarrassed because we don't have the answers we think we should have. We rarely admit to anyone (especially our children) that we're insecure. Some of us are even brazen enough to write books and newspaper columns about child rearing despite the fact that we're insecure. So remember, underneath what may be a big or powerful exterior, there's a little boy or girl inside scratching his head saying, "Geez, I don't know what to do either" (don't expect us to admit this to you; it's too embarrassing).

- Our hearing is defective. Most of us hear the voices of our parents, our bosses, our spouses, and our consciences saying things like, "You must make more money," "You must look better," "Your children must be well-behaved," "You must get in shape," "You must get a promotion," and on and on and on. Try to imagine all that noise inside the head of a person who is already insecure (and also has had something removed from their brain by that sucking machine!). Therefore, it is very difficult for us to listen to your wishes, frustrations, or demands. It's even more difficult to hear what's really going on inside your heart. Because we have these defects, you have to work extra hard to help us understand your thoughts, desires, and needs.

- Our vision is also impaired. As we get older we look at things like clothes, furniture, and bankbooks and start to think things like that are important. We sometimes forget that the important things to look at are leaves, frogs, ducks, and ants making an anthill. You'll have to help us remember that. And please, please be patient—sometimes we learn something and forget it very quickly. So, you'll have to teach it to us again and again.

- As we get older, some of us tend to get rigid. To be honest, I'm really not sure why this is. It might have to do with the missing "stuff" or the fact that we get more nervous and insecure as we age, and being rigid helps us feel like our world is safer and more organized. I'll bet you do the same when you're scared; you dig in your heels and act stronger and smarter than you really feel.

- When we get into trouble, you have to let us work it out for ourselves or else we'll never grow up! Several years ago, a young man about 20 years old came to see me along with his parents. He complained that they fought frequently, and he kept getting involved in their arguments; taking one side or the other—trying to make them happy. I advised him to use a new technique that I recently patented called "Zie Gezhint Therapy!" ("Zie Gezhint" is a yiddish phrase meaning "live and be well"). We usually use this phrase right after we say goodbye to someone. I advised him when his parents began to fight, to hold up his hands, say "zie gezhint," turn around, and walk out of the room. He called me several months later to tell me how well my new "therapy" had worked. (By the way, his parents said it worked well for them, too.)

You see, at a certain point you have to realize, you've raised us the best you could; and you'll have to let us go and fend for ourselves.

But remember, 20, 30, or 40 years from now—we'll be back.

Trying To Help When A 13-Year-Old Daughter's Personality Changes

Dear Dr. Gottlieb:

I am concerned about my 13-year-old daughter. She has just entered eighth grade and seems to have had a personality change. Previously, she was outgoing, loved sports, had good grades, many friends, and seemed to enjoy life. Recently, however, she is withdrawn and isolated. She spends most of her time alone in her room.

Are these the normal changes that go with puberty, or should I be concerned about her?

A Concerned Mother

Dear Concerned Mother:

Puberty is a very difficult stage of life for all children. With it comes a shift in identity and the beginning of a change from childhood to adulthood. Much of this shift has to do with their changing bodies and everything that goes with it. This generally marks the beginning of adult sexuality, which can be both frightening and exciting. As a result, boys and girls begin to relate to one another differently. The pressure can be pretty difficult for adolescent children.

If you think back to when you were 13, I'm sure it was anything but comfortable. Many are ashamed or frightened of these new changes and may feel out of control. One logical way for them to cope is to do what your daughter is doing—hide in their rooms.

This happens to both boys and girls. However, we have recently discovered that the effect of puberty is very different and can be much more painful for girls. Research done by the American Association of University Women, several years ago, demonstrated that girls' self-esteem is generally good before age 10. They are as self-confident and accomplished as boys at this age. When they emerge from puberty, their self-confidence drops, they become less assertive, and tend to be more shy and withdrawn.

I contacted Dr. Emily Hancock, a psychologist in Berkeley, California, who wrote *The Girl Within* (Fawcett), which describes this phenomenon. I asked her to comment on what might be happening with your daughter.

She explained, "Research tells us that generally girls up until age 10 are pretty focused, energized, and enjoy life. They feel good about themselves and their influence and have an appropriate sense of power both in their families and among their peers. However, when girls go into puberty and their bodies change, so does the world around them.

"Our society tells these girls that instead of being valued for their brains, their assertiveness, their personality; they're now valued for these new and developing bodies. In order to 'make it' in this new world, girls often lose their previous identity and self-confidence. They're taught by our society that the only way they can be successful as women is to be pretty and compliant. Their personality and skills aren't as valuable as their beauty and grace.

"Also, at this stage, their families, which may have been quite supportive and encouraging of their old identity, begin to have less influence as peers begin to play a more dominant role. Boys, who used to be the same size as they, are now bigger and more powerful, physically and emotionally. Now, all of a sudden, the boys and even men in their environments are looking not in their eyes but at their bodies. What they see in their future is that men get bigger, relatively; and women get smaller."

I asked Hancock what could be done to help your daughter through such a difficult time. "Her mother and father must understand that the women who are portrayed in our culture are facsimiles and not real women. They are airbrushed images. Her father must resist the tendency that many fathers have to withdraw when their daughters begin to develop. He must hang in there and become her enabler.

"Girls often see their father as the link to the outside world. Therefore, if she had dreams of being a doctor or an archaeologist, her father could help her research that. Mother, of course, could do the same thing; but it is critical that she communicate to her daughter that what she sees in magazines and on TV about women is just not right."

I believe all of us, in order to become socialized, must lose parts of ourselves. If we're lucky, the parts we lose are the "rough edges." Too often, however, many of us lose parts that make up our very fabric. What we wind up with then is men and women who are highly socialized and, yet, unhappy. We see women who complain because they give too much of themselves to others, and men who complain because they work too hard. I believe that many of these problems come from the fact that their childhood voices and personalities have been silenced for so many years. For most of us, it's difficult to go back and reclaim the dreams, clarity of thinking, and self-confidence we had when we were children. But, I promise you that the voice is still in there.

The bright light that was your daughter's personality has begun to flicker. To maintain its brightness, it needs help from you and her father. Make sure you know what is important both in your daughter and yourselves. After all is said and done, we learn that faces and bodies change over the years; therefore, it's the beauty of the character that we must cherish.

Rules; An Essential For Substance Abusers

Dear Dr. Gottlieb:

My son-in-law developed a compulsive behavior in various aspects of life. This culminated in recent years in excessive spending for equipment in his business, ending in bankruptcy, drug use (crack), and sexual addiction. Through my daughter's insistence, he spent 2 ½ months in a rehab environment before he quit and has been living again with his family (two daughters, 7 and 10). He relapsed into crack use once.

Now they are coming to live with me. I would be grateful for some advice on how to deal with him, what would be supportive for better development, and how to set boundaries.

Dear Reader:

As I'm sure you know, substance abuse is a chronic disease for which there is no known cure. The risk of relapse is ever present; but the longer the period of sobriety, the smaller the chances for relapse. As you describe your son-in-law, he seems to be a very fragile substance abuser who, despite what may be a commitment to his rehabilitation, is at risk for relapse. There are certain specifics that should be done before anyone invites a substance abuser to live with him or her. This list is not exhaustive and must be tailored to fit your family:

- Insist he be in ongoing treatment while he lives with you (at least three Narcotics Anonymous meetings a week, individual and/or group psychotherapy, etc.). In addition, it would be a mistake to trust his word. There must be evidence that he completes this.

- Make sure both your daughter and her husband are treated like mature, responsible adults. Negotiate appropriate and reasonable financial arrangements with them. If you can afford it, perhaps you could give them a grace period to find work. After that, work out a reasonable and realistic room-and-board fee. To do otherwise would be to enable them to be dependent and irresponsible.
- Work out clear arrangements for the children. If you can, and if you would like to, it would be wonderful to help your daughter and son-in-law with the children. Just keep in mind, they need to be the primary caretakers. If you take responsibility for the children, it may enable their parents to be less responsible (not to mention putting an extra burden on you).
- Your daughter and son-in-law must understand that if there is a relapse, the consequence will be eviction (or whatever you deem appropriate). Keep in mind, it is not your responsibility to monitor his sobriety; but if he is visibly intoxicated or behaving irresponsibly, he must be held accountable.
- I strongly suggest your husband, daughter, and you go to Al-Anon or Nar-Anon for families of substance abusers. They will support you and help you focus on yourself and your own welfare. Most importantly, they will help you establish boundaries.

If these limits and boundaries can be clearly established before they move in, it will take pressure off all of you. Once everyone knows the rules, you can be freer to support, love, and nurture this family in ways that fit your own value system.

Once boundaries are established and rules and roles are clear, I would suggest all of you (those directly involved and not) get involved in family therapy. It may be helpful for everyone to be able to talk about the many important issues and emotions that accompany issues of substance abuse.

Can Parents Force Son, 20, To Seek Help?

Dear Dr. Gottlieb:

My husband and I are in dire need of help. Can our 20-year-old son, who lives at home, be forced to get help for depression?

His problems surfaced in elementary school when teachers began complaining of excessive fidgeting at his desk, getting out of his seat, inability to focus, and so on. He was diagnosed with Attention Deficit Disorder (ADD), put in special education classes, and prescribed Ritalin. He remained on Ritalin about a year and a half. We discontinued Ritalin after he complained that it was not working even though the dosage had been increased.

Basically, high school was a disaster for him. He hated school, and we became weary of the telephone calls and notes from concerned teachers. His last year in high school was punctuated with detentions and uncooperative behavior.

The school authorities took it upon themselves to have him schooled at home two weeks before graduation. He was too disruptive to remain in school. But prior to the home schooling, he made a threat of suicide, which the school took seriously. He was barred from returning to school unless he was seen by an outside counselor. He was diagnosed with depression, and Prozac and counseling sessions were prescribed. Again, it proved a disaster. He refused to cooperate with the counselor, clamming up at the sessions. He complained that the Prozac was not working. Zoloft was prescribed; after a week he refused to take it.

My husband I finally threw in the towel and discontinued the counseling. His attitude and behavior continued to spiral downhill, particularly to his older brother and us.

Since graduation, his life has gone into a free fall. He has become increasingly more angry, defiant, and disrespectful toward his father and me. If allowed, he will sleep all day and stay up all night.

Attempts at employment were few and resulted in firing. His sole interest, in illustrating in the Japanese anime (animation) style, is gone. Use of marijuana and alcohol has increased as his depression has deepened. We have put him out of the house on a number of occasions because of his belligerent behavior toward us. The last time was for a month, and he spent most of that time in the streets.

We love him and care deeply about him, but we are emotionally and mentally spent. We also know that he is hurting, too.

This Friday, my husband and I will attend an Al-Anon meeting. That's a start, but what do we do next?

Worried Parents

Dear Parents:

Unfortunately, you are not alone in your struggle. I hear from too many parents that they are caring for their grown children who seem out of control. Your problems are twofold: One is what is going on with your son; the other is how to cope with his behavior. The brief amount of information you have given is certainly not enough to formulate a diagnosis. But it is enough to suggest possibilities.

Certainly there is probably depression and possible ADD and substance abuse. The one possibility that was not mentioned is a Bipolar Disorder. If possible, I would recommend that your son see a psychiatrist or psychologist, who can evaluate him for manic-depressive illness, also called Bipolar Disorder. His childhood agitation and belligerent behavior could be symptoms of the manic phase of the illness. It is also possible that he is using marijuana and alcohol to try to control the agitation (many substance abusers use drugs and alcohol to try to quiet the "demons" inside). Although this is a serious diagnosis, treatment is available. Many people with Bipolar Disorder show remarkable improvement with psychotherapy and medications. There are also support groups available for loved ones.

Many parents who have children with mental illness feel guilty and responsible. It is important to know that Bipolar Disorder is a brain disorder that is primarily influenced by genetics; not caused by family stresses. If he agrees to be evaluated, it is very possible that, in a strange way, a diagnosis like this could be a relief. It could be the end of your anger, fear, and frustration with his behavior and could restore some of your compassion. It could also help your son as I would imagine he has feelings of shame and low self-esteem. Knowing that he has a brain disorder could help him feel less bad about himself.

Realistically, though, you have to look at the possibility that he will refuse to be evaluated. Whether he agrees or not, your decision to seek the support of groups such as Al-Anon or Nar-Anon is a good idea. If you find a group you are comfortable with, it can help you learn how to love and care about your son but not take responsibility for his behavior. The group will also give you the tools and the support to set limits on his behavior so his illness does not have to control your life also.

Whether he goes for an evaluation is up to him—your influence is minimal. The best you can do is withdraw whatever you have been doing that enables him to continue his lifestyle. Other than that, your influence is restricted to wishes and prayers.

For further reading, I suggest *An Unquiet Mind* (Knopf) by Kay Redfield Jamison.

Forced Treatment Not Option For Parents

I recently wrote about two parents concerned for their 20-year old son. According to their letter, he displayed a lifetime of emotional problems and had shown symptoms of substance abuse. He was refusing help, and his parents wanted to know if he could be forced into treatment. I suggested they have their son evaluated for Bipolar Disorder and encouraged them to set their own boundaries in the event he refused to be evaluated. A reader offered another approach.

Dear Dr. Gottlieb:

I hope you are not offended if I say that your column, while instructive and accurate, was not responsive to the question posed by "Worried Parents." Having spent years with our own son, (somewhat older and he not having any pre-onset history), my wife and I know that the answer to the question posed in the opening paragraph ("Can parents force son, 20, to seek help?") is an unfortunate and simple "No."

Our experience introduced us to the whole unfortunate legal system surrounding a 302 commitment for treatment....Several times, we found ourselves having to make the painful decision to have our son involuntarily hospitalized. Incidentally, these hospitalizations always led to stabilization followed by eventual non-compliance with his medication after a period of "wellness."

Our story, though, is a success because after his fifth confinement in his fifth hospital, he finally accepted that he might need medication for the rest of his life. Since then, he has made a complete turnaround, [became] gainfully employed in a good situation worthy of his talents, and was able to get off Social Security. Our son is now living a full life, and I admire his courage in having fought through this terrible and protracted ordeal.

I write because I truly believe "Worried Parents" should have a more direct response to their question, one that holds out hope that if they choose this very difficult path, they could have a positive outcome.

Dear Reader:

I always appreciate constructive criticism, and your advice may be helpful to other readers, although I don't think "Worried Parents" have the options you did.

Commitment laws are very carefully designed to protect both patients and society. If it is too easy to commit someone, then angry or frustrated parents could have a loved one "put away" just for being stubborn and irritating. Such was the case historically when involuntary commitment was relatively easy. Of course, this created civil rights problems for prospective patients that ultimately put everybody at risk.

According to Alex Siegel, forensic psychologist at Delaware Valley Behavioral Health in Philadelphia, most states have developed simple criteria for involuntary hospitalization; "For adults, they must have a diagnosable mental illness other than substance abuse, and they must be a danger to themselves or others."

But to further ensure simple rights, the courts will not simply take the word of another person. "The prospective patient must have shown clear evidence within the last 30 days that they have been actively suicidal and have been a danger to themselves or to others," Siegel explained. "If that's the case, then one can petition the courts for a 72-hour involuntary commitment for evaluation. However, even if the courts approve a commitment, a patient's managed-care company could still deny payment."

Siegel went on to explain that this narrow interpretation could make life very difficult for family members as well as mental health professionals. Our society tends to err on the side of civil rights. In light of that, I don't believe "Worried Parents" have the option of involuntary commitment available to them.

In addition, your experience might be the exception. To protect civil rights, involuntary hospitalization is almost always brief—often just a few days. Therefore, all that can realistically be expected is to interrupt dangerous behavior and begin appropriate medication. If these hospitals had more time and resources, patient and family would also have a course of psychotherapy. Psychotherapy may not cure a major mental illness, but it can help understand and diminish the shame that, unfortunately, goes with mental illness. If patients and family understand that mental illness is a disorder of the brain and that medication can help keep it under control, the chances of recovery are greatly improved.

Involuntary hospitalization though is a double-edged sword. Certainly, if a loved one is a danger to self or others, he or she must be forced into treatment. But, isolation and alienation are potentially lethal by-products of mental illness; forcing someone to do something could save a life or could make the sense of isolation worse.

I'm glad things worked out so well for you. Perhaps more people could get the results you did if our hospitals had the funding and the staffing to provide top quality treatment for those who need it most.

Persistent Longing For Son To Know Father

Dear Dr. Gottlieb,

My son recently had his seventh birthday. There was so much I wanted to say to him and didn't know how. I have difficulty sorting out my feelings let alone expressing them. The look that I saw on my son's face reminded me of how I felt when I was seven years old and looked at my father. We never quite connected—despite all my efforts to be the boy I thought he wanted me to be.

Now it's 35 years later, and my father is aging. We watch baseball games together and my wish to connect is still there. Every time we try to talk, however, we wind up arguing; the subject matter is irrelevant. It seems that we argue over anything but sports. I'm concerned that I will lose him, never having really known him. I don't know how to get him to talk about his feelings; nor do I know how to talk about mine.

How do we begin the process? The relationship feels so empty.

Bill

Dear Bill,

The father-son relationship is one of the most difficult in the family. There are so many men I speak with who long for a closer relationship with their fathers. How does this happen?

Author and poet Robert Bly suggests that it all started with the Industrial Revolution. Things were fine as long as Dad stayed on the farm. When the "revolution" came, he left early in the morning and came home at night after the children were asleep. Even when the children were up, he was too tired to talk to them about anything, let alone his feelings. In modern days, we men either are made to feel shameful about expressing our emotions, or are socialized to repress them, to associate feelings with weakness. Bill, we've been duped!

After generations of withholding intimate feelings, it now becomes awkward and embarrassing to try to express them to anybody, let alone your father! To explore some options of dealing with these uncomfortable emotions, I shared your letter with Dr. Meyer Rothbart, a psychiatrist in the Philadelphia suburbs, who is known for his use of therapeutic humor. Here's what he said:

"It's clear to me from your letter that you value intimate relationships, and you would like to be more effectively loving. My own father was from an Eastern European culture while I was brought up in the United States. The rules of his era were not effective in mine. I also did not feel comfortable with American role models for men. I felt very much on my own and had to learn for myself what it meant to be a loving man. I did not like admitting that I had to learn the basics, but I took my task very seriously. Somehow I knew I had to regain the capacities of the playful boy I sometimes was.

"Help came from unexpected quarters. As a child and adult, I never liked clowns, yet I was shocked to find out that it was joyful and outrageous to dress up as a clown—makeup and all. I discovered that when I dressed up, the whole world looked like my playground and people looked like my playmates.

"I felt an unusual kind of freedom for the first time in my adult life. It even affected my professional life. As a clown I could experience myself as a playful little boy with adult judgment. I could use friendly humor for my own health and the health of my patients. As a father and husband, I could better relate to feelings—the 'inner child' in others and myself.

"When it comes to intimate feelings, many of us feel like a fool. When I do, I dress 'him' up like a clown, and he gets accepted by others and myself. I found friendly humor and clowning so meaningful that I taught it to my teenage son, and we do workshops together on clowning and humor. I feel it has brought us much closer.

"It is the natural instinct of the psyche to seek wholeness; expressing your feelings and your wish to know your father are consistent with that instinct. Humor is one way to deal with these issues."

Perhaps you could tell your father about your wish and your awkwardness. It's risky, but it might make your dad feel safer (yes, he needs to feel safe too). No matter what happens, if you have the courage to face your father with your hunger and your fear, your relationship with your own son will benefit.

What Hurts Our Children, And What Helps

Like everybody else, I was terribly upset about the massacre of 12 schoolchildren and a teacher in Littleton, Colorado. But, we don't need another psychologist theorizing about the killers and their families. What might be helpful, though, is talking about what harms children, what helps them, and what we can do.

Things that harm children:

• Neglect and abuse. Some adults are too injured or depleted to adequately care for children.

- Poverty. More and more research shows poverty contributes to low self-esteem, a feeling of hopelessness and depression.
- Chronic parental illness; whether physical or emotional. Even an unhappy or pessimistic parent can interfere with a child's healthy development.
- Poor education. Besides facing future academic and social difficulties, children with less achievement in school feel as though they are not part of the larger world.
- Lack of community support. Much research shows that children can compensate for inadequate parenting if there are alternatives. If not, feelings of isolation and alienation are likely to occur.
- Repeated criticism by parents or teachers. Children, who are repeatedly judged negatively or punished, eventually will begin to see themselves as bad or inadequate. Frequently, a child who feels beaten down by the external world will act aggressively.
- Exposure to hatred. Few things harm children more. Children learn hatred and tolerance of violence from a variety of sources including television and their families. Hatred can seem acceptable when adults pass judgment on whole groups of people or blame them for others' problems.
- Alienation. When children feel neglected or misunderstood, they will feel alienated. Children who are talked to, but not listened to, will also feel that way. When I hear a parent say, "I know my child better than he knows himself," I usually find a child who feels alienated.

Other things that hurt children are divorce, absent fathers, a parent's loss of employment, and frequent change of residence or school.

What helps children?

- Predictable, caring relationships. They are of primary importance, according to virtually every study on this topic. Supportive people contribute to a child's sense of safety and well being.
- Realistically high expectations and achievement orientation. If we expect too little, children will perform accordingly. If we expect too

much, they will become frustrated and feel inadequate. The task is to shape our expectations around our children's competencies, not around our own desires for them.

• Extended family bonds and community involvement. Children, who have access to more resources than just the immediate family, tend to have a better sense of themselves and do better in later life.

• Family unity. Children can flourish in a family that is purposeful and goal-oriented; a family with mutual respect and understanding; a family that understands its role and responsibility to the immediate community and larger world.

• Ability to contribute. Children do well when they feel they have the ability and an opportunity to contribute to the welfare of others. This is why older siblings who have taken care of younger siblings tend to be more resilient after a trauma.

• Faith. Children are happier if they have a sense of spiritual trust, of being part of something universal.

• Eye contact. Children probably never feel alienated if people care enough to look into their eyes and see into their hearts.

What we can do:

Most parents I know are doing a fine job with their children. Maybe the parents worry a bit too much, or work too hard, and could spend some more time with their children. Overall, though, they do a fine job.

But most parents fail to show their children that they are an essential part of the larger community. Parents typically don't get involved in helping others who need help the most. Therefore, their children grow up with an isolationist mentality. And isolationism breeds alienation and anxiety.

Many people complain that they feel helpless to do anything about youth violence and alienation. But a study conducted by Big Brothers and Big Sisters of America found that children who met with their big brother or big sister about three times a month for at least a year, when compared to a control group, were 56 percent less likely to begin using illegal drugs and 37 percent less likely to begin using alcohol.

Schools are another resource. If you want to be part of the solution, give a few hours a week to your local school. I have felt for years that schools should work like a cooperative. Every parent who sends a child should automatically donate a few hours a week. Just think about how much extra attention and caring the children would get. If our schools had more adults with open hearts, they might have fewer children with loaded guns.

Chapter 4...Our Emotions

Quick To Anger; Wants To Slow Up

Dear Dr. Gottlieb,

We all have things we don't like about ourselves, and I don't like my quickness to anger. Today, I walked into a crowded luncheonette to pick up a sandwich. A man walked in after me, and the waitress offered to help him first. I fumed inside. I took her aside and told her angrily that I came in first. She apologized, and I felt embarrassed about my anger.

Last week someone walking her dog left a "present" in the middle of our sidewalk. I became furious, gathered it in plastic bags, and drove around the neighborhood trying to find her. I never found her, but I was very angry that someone would leave that in the center of our sidewalk. We have kids in the neighborhood, and we live across from a church. I would hate to see the "present" on the rugs inside our church.

What really bothers me, though, is my quickness to anger in such situations. Is there any way I could react less strongly?

Unnamed and Embarrassed

Dear Unnamed and Embarrassed,

You are certainly not alone. I believe our whole society has difficulty dealing with anger. Murder and rape are magnified expressions of such anger. Proliferating lawsuits are expressions of anger; and if you look at our most recent elections, much of the campaign rhetoric sounded like angry young children calling each other names. Even the outcome of the election says something about how angry we are. We elected people who would provide more prisons, longer prison terms, more death penalties, fewer social programs, and a bigger military. Again, social expressions of anger.

On the flip side, a good deal of research suggests depression, hypertension, some cardiovascular problems, and many ulcerative conditions are made worse by anger held inside and unexpressed. So on one hand we have a group of people who always seem to be baring their teeth; and on the other, we have the angry, silent types who may be depressed or have stomach cramps!

This really raises two questions. Why is there so much anger, and why do we have so much trouble expressing it appropriately?

Anger is usually a healthy and adaptive emotion. It keeps us alert and responsive when we feel we, or our loved ones, are threatened. But why does everyone seem so angry at times? After all, most of us have decent jobs and homes and enough money to feed and clothe our families.

Well, anger is also a reactive emotion. Anger is a typical reaction to physical or emotional injury or even anticipated injury. Usually, when you see anger, you're seeing someone who has been hurt.

To take your letter at face value, your anger, like the anger we see in society, seems to make no sense. After all, your life wasn't threatened in either incident; so why would you react as though it was?

Let's look at these incidents from the perspective of your psyche. In order to do this, we must understand that your psyche is blind, deaf, and mute; all it can do is feel—how it perceives things depends on its history and its genetics. For example, I noticed both of the incidents you described were violations of your boundaries (the first one your personal boundaries; the second one your community boundaries). I wonder if you are especially vigilant about boundary violations. Were your boundaries violated in the past? Perhaps you had an intrusive or violent parent or sibling or maybe privacy was hard to find.

If you've been hurt frequently, either as a child or adult, you will tend to be more vigilant and "ready" to attack. In addition, if someone in your family had a quick temper, you may be prone to have one too.

Now let's go back into the luncheonette as a psyche who has no voice; who has been wounded; who might be feeling fragile, frightened or threatened. Now, instead of seeing yourself as an angry or volatile person, let's begin to see you as a vulnerable person who has been hurt and continues to feel frightened of repeated attacks. Because you have long antennae, you are ever vigilant, and prepared to protect yourself. You may "see" the slightest violation (e.g., a person cutting in front of you in line) as an attack.

The question remains: Why is it so difficult to express anger appropriately? Whenever there is anger in the picture, there is always hurt and fear. When we are able to understand that anger is about injury and vulnerability, it becomes less threatening and, therefore, easier to express. We can say things like "That hurts, please don't do it to me;" or "I was here first and I'm in a rush, please wait;" or "Don't do that in my neighborhood."

As far as treatment is concerned, there are a variety of things that can be done for people who have difficulty with anger. First is to understand, tolerate, and respect the sense of injury that underlies the angry reaction. If this process is done in psychotherapy, a competent mental health professional will take you back through your history to help you understand what caused you this pain and resulting anger. This should help you be less vigilant. Another alternative is cognitive therapy. In this approach, the therapist helps you understand the overactive thoughts that may get triggered by these violations. It is often these irrational thoughts that lead to the extreme feelings and behavior. A cognitive therapist can help you understand and modify these thoughts. A third option (and this should be used in conjunction with one of the first two) is medication. There is some evidence that some of the newer antidepressants can help put a coat of "Teflon" on your nerve endings so you become less reactive to what happens in your environment. Although this may work in the short run, it should be integrated with psychotherapy to maintain the gains you've made.

Trying To Figure Out Source Of A Caller's Anxiety Disorder

"Hello, Dr. Gottlieb, could you give me some advice?" the caller said. "I'm a 65 year-old woman, I've been married for 40 years, and have a grown son who is getting along in life quite well. I, too, have always been productive; I've worked, had hobbies, and friends. There's only one small problem that interferes with my ability to enjoy my life; I have always been too concerned about tomorrow. I can't focus on today as I worry about tomorrow's duties and responsibilities."

"How long has this been going on?" I asked, wondering whether something had recently happened that might have triggered her anxiety about the future and the obsessive thinking. (Something like the sudden death of a loved one or similar trauma could be the culprit.)

"It seems I've been a worrier my whole life," she said, "but lately it's been getting worse."

Given her age, this made me wonder whether it was partly a life-cycle issue. Sometimes when we face our mortality, we find it's easier to look at tomorrow's tasks rather than today's truths.

Next, I wondered whether there were any patterns that could teach us something about her problem. I asked her whether there were any times in her life when she was free of these thoughts or times when they were worse. This could help us understand, not just the cause of these thoughts, but also what could contribute to diminishing them.

"There have been times when it's better, like when I swim or exercise, but basically it's pretty consistent," she said.

I then began to wonder about the endorphins in her brain. These are the hormones that, among other things, make us feel good. They have been called the body's "natural opiates," and they often get released with exercise. That information raised a question in my mind about the possibility of medication because that, too, works on brain chemistry. But before I recommended she see a psychopharmacologist, I wanted to know more about her.

I asked whether she had ever been in therapy.

"I've tried counseling before," she said, "but they simply want to probe in my past, and I don't want to."

"Why don't you want to," I asked, wondering whether she had feelings or some history that were too difficult or repressed.

"It doesn't seem relevant; I had a good family with no traumas. It seems the therapist I saw just assumed that the problem was in my past, I saw it differently, so therapy didn't work."

I knew this was true. If patient and therapist can't agree on some basic assumptions about the problem, its cause and direction of treatment, therapy won't work.

Before I made a recommendation, I wanted her to understand her problem in context. It's helpful to see where a problem fits in our lives rather than seeing the problem or symptom as having a life of its own. So I asked her to think about the overall picture of her life.

"Not just the tasks for tomorrow," I said, "but how your life is and where you see it going. Be aware of your feelings as you do this exercise, as it could be frightening, painful, or sad. Sometimes focusing on one thing helps us avoid looking at something that might be even more distressing. This knowledge will help you understand where the work needs to be done. It may also help diminish the power of the distressing thoughts."

As she thought about her life, I thought about what I'd learned from her and how I could be most helpful. There are a variety of ways to deal with this kind of situation. Fortunately, many anxiety disorders (that is the technical name for what I think she was suffering with) generally have a good prognosis. Counseling could be helpful to her, and not all counseling requires a long and tedious look at a person's past. Some forms work almost exclusively with what's happening right now, and some are quite active.

That's the good news. The bad news is that not all mental health professionals know how to treat an anxiety disorder. It requires successful training. Dr. Linda Welsh of the Agoraphobia and Anxiety Treatment Center in Bala Cynwyd, PA offered these thoughts:

- The most important task for people under stress is to examine their lives and try to diminish the stress.
- It is also important to explore the fear behind the obsessive thoughts. In this woman's case it would be helpful to understand what would happen if she didn't "take care" of tomorrow's tasks. This information could help determine the proper treatment.
- Sometimes obsessive thoughts are a result of early trauma. There are new treatments available, however, that can tackle the specific trauma. These treatments are short term and show a great deal of promise.
- Most importantly, a person may need to find a therapist with behavioral training to teach him or her coping skills to manage anxiety and obsessive thoughts. These skills include learning to relax muscles that will calm breathing, focusing on the present, and stopping certain thoughts.
- Medication can sometimes be useful; but, first, a proper diagnosis must be made. When medication is indicated, it works best in conjunction with therapy.

Compassion

Compassion. It can end most arguments, and it could cure alienation. Compassion is simply understanding the experience of another person and feeling care and kindness for them. It could change the world. Apparently babies and small children do this quite well. Regardless of gender, when a baby is in the presence of another baby who is crying, they also cry. Young children can feel terribly distressed if one of their friends is hurt or sad.

Young children have compassion, but with adults it is more difficult to find. It seems compassion starts to dissipate during the elementary school years.

In one column, I wrote about my visit to a suburban junior high school where I spoke with nearly 200 students. I described how one of their major concerns was being "put down" by other students. Approximately half said they had they had been on the receiving end of what they described as a terribly hurtful and embarrassing experience. That's why I was surprised by the response I got when I asked them how many of them "put down" other students. Nearly everyone raised his or her hand! I wondered why knowing how hurtful this behavior is could they continue to do it to other students? And where was the compassion?

I contacted Genie Silver, a psychologist who teaches "Behavior and Ethics in Conflict and War" at Villanova University's Center for Peace and Justice Education. She explained that it is almost inevitable that one person will see another through a lens of bias, "Most people have a reservoir of anger and other emotions inside because of past hurts or injustice. But, not just our own experience with hurt and injustice, we frequently carry the hurt and injustice of our parents and community. So when we meet new or different people, it is very hard to see them for who they really are. We bring our inherited prejudices with us."

So, it's a simple fact. We see one another through a lens of our family, our genetics, and our own experiences. As a result, we rarely see one another with the empathy and compassion we had when we were children.

Silver went on to explain that the distortions tend to get worse when we deal with people who are "different." "When we first counter someone from a different ethnic group or economic background, we are more likely to see them through a lens of hurt or fear; and we will see them as potential enemies or threats."

Most violence occurs when one feels threatened or insecure. When one feels threatened, he or she may become aggressive. The person they lash out at then feels threatened, insecure, and may also become aggressive. This cycle of insecurity and aggression may have contributed to the violence at Columbine and other schools around the country. Silver went on to explain some of the elements in this cycle that could culminate in violence; "From what little we know about the students who committed the violence at Columbine, we know that they were alienated and angry. We also know that the vast majority of the students heckled them at one time or another. These boys felt threatened by their fellow students, and their fellow students probably felt threatened by them. I also believe there was no one in their environment who took the time to try to understand them, which may have diffused the situation."

Compassion diminishes anger because anger is a judicial emotion. Most of the time, anger is a natural reaction to injustice. And, caring about the experience of others diminishes one's sense of injustice. Think about it. When we are treated unjustly, we always feel better when we are with someone who is willing and able to understand our experience.

Compassion.

All of this sounds good, but it's not that easy. How can one feel compassion for a person or group which has caused them injury? Sometimes it can be done. But other times…

A story: A Zen master was mugged at gunpoint one night on a city street. Stripped of all of his belongings, he left feeling violated, angry, and resentful. Being human, his first instinct was to seek safety; his second was to seek revenge. But, by the time he got to the monastery, he felt quite differently. He told the story of what happened to a colleague and then began to cry. Through his tears he explained, "If I had lived the life that man had lived, if I had his family and his experiences, I would have been the man with the gun. And if he had lived my history, he would have been blessed with my wonderful life. How terribly sad for him."

As our children grow and become socialized, they lose compassion. That's because they live in a world that has little time to learn about the experience of another person but, instead, passes judgment on their lives or behavior in the name of "values." Too busy and too judgmental for compassion.

But compassion can be taught. When your child talks about a fellow student, ask them to guess about what that student must feel like. When watching television and someone gets hurt, ask what their loved ones must be feeling. When you are out in public and someone is begging for money, talk with your child about what it must feel like to not have a home. The world is full of ways to teach compassion. If the next generation has more compassion, the world will see less conflict.

That Nagging Unhappiness Might Be A Cry Of The Spirit For Renewal

Dear Dan,

A recent column about people needing to have meaning in their lives struck a cord with me. I am a 46 year-old woman with a decent job. My marriage is not exciting or passionate, but my husband is a nice man. The children are grown; the youngest left home three years ago. This all sounds fine; but for years I have had what I call a "low-grade depression," a nagging unhappiness that something is missing in my life. As I age, this feeling troubles me more.

Over the years I've tried everything I could think of to ease this. For years, I drank to excess. As I'm sure you know, it only worked temporarily; then, things got worse. I tried going back to school thinking lack of education was the problem. I went on retreats, explored massage, and special diets. Years ago, I even had an affair thinking what I needed was more passion in my life. That didn't work either.

I've been in therapy twice and tried medication, but nothing seems to work. I'm still left with this dull ache inside. For some reason, your column spoke to me. I've looked to heal my mind and body, but maybe the spirit needs attention. And if I'm right, what do I do about it?

Linda

Dear Linda,

There is a possibility your "low-grade depression" is just that. The technical name is "Dysthymia." It's generally treated quite successfully with psychotherapy provided there is a good match between you and the therapist.

Even if that is the case, it could be there is something missing spiritually. After all, I don't think it's a coincidence that the alcohol you drank to excess is often referred to as "spirits." As a matter of fact, at a recent conference on spirituality and healing sponsored by Harvard University, pollster George Gallup, Jr., reported 9 in 10 people who are recovering from addiction attribute their success to a religious or spiritual conversion.

Spirituality comes naturally to children. They have faith. Most have faith in the benevolence of their parents. The majority also believes in the presence of G-d who created a meaningful universe. Because of their faith, they believe they will be okay in this world.

As they grow, many people lose their faith. They become distracted by matters of the ego; their looks, power, beauty, and achievement. They also get involved in the realities of a busy life; relationships, child rearing, and career building. In mid-life, when people may be losing their looks or power and their accomplishments no longer bring satisfaction, they often feel that something is missing.

Carl Jung said the first half of One's life is about matters of the ego; the second half is when we become aware that our history is longer than our future; and that one day, sooner than we might wish, our lives will be over. So, we look for meaning and often divine guidance.

At the Harvard conference, Gallup also reported that 9 in 10 people already believe G-d is in their lives. If so, then why are addiction rates increasing, and why do so many people feel bereft of spirituality? Apparently, many people believe in G-d. They just don't trust G-d; belief, but no faith.

We know that people who have faith and pray regularly tend to be happier and have a better outlook on life. Some scientists believe the act of prayer is like meditation and is good for both mind and body.

But maybe it's not that simple. At the same conference, Larry Dossey and Marilyn Schlitz presented evidence that prayer has a measurable effect on those who receive prayer. In a controlled study involving 393 people admitted to a coronary care unit, half were prayed for by people of faith. The people who did the praying were at a geographic distance, and the patients they prayed for didn't know in which group they were. The patients who were prayed for had significantly fewer complications and left the hospital earlier than the other group.

Sometimes faith comes and goes in our lives, and suffering can become an opportunity to renew it. Three years ago, I became terribly despondent after being confined to bed for several months. I told a friend who was visiting that I didn't know if I had the emotional strength to endure this suffering; that if my life were to end that day, it would be okay. She touched my arm and said: "You are here for a purpose. That purpose is more important than who you are."

Something about those words touched me deeply; and, that night, I had the following dream: Three spiritual men came to me and produced a mink-brown butterfly. "This is your soul," one said. "You must inhale it to become a complete person". The butterfly looked about 3 inches in diameter. "I can't," I said, "I'll choke, and I might die." "That's not so important," he said. "You must do it in order to be whole." I put it in my mouth

—and woke up. The message? Sometimes we must let go of life in order to save it.

I'll pray for you, Linda. It may do us both some good.

One Can Be A Very Lonely Number When The Holidays Roll Around

Dear Dr. Gottlieb:

I'm a 47 year-old single woman living alone. I enjoy my work that I find interesting and challenging, have good friends, a brother, and a mother; all of who love me. These are people with whom I can share both the important and the daily events of my life. I have my own home, which I love and enough income. I even have the time to be involved in volunteer work with people I like. I have most of what I want in life and am mostly satisfied.

My question is about living with the loneliness I sometimes feel. This loneliness ranges from the sense of isolation I feel when I haven't been touched or held, to the emptiness of my house or bed, to an ache that seems to come from my very core. Sometimes I busy my way through these lonely times; and sometimes I do something mindless like eat, watch TV, or bury myself in a good mystery. And, sometimes, if I'm not feeling too raw, I can call a friend and say, "I'm lonely."

For many years, I've wanted to be married or in some other form of an intimate relationship; but for a variety of reasons, my relationships never worked out. At this stage in my life, I'm starting to believe that being alone may be permanent.

The pain is so much worse during the holidays when it seems that everyone is in a relationship. In addition to the pain of being alone during these times, I feel almost defective.

Sarah

Dear Sarah:

There are many kinds of loneliness. Philosophers write about existential loneliness. This is the loneliness that comes with being human, and it begins in childhood. Many children experience this loneliness when they realize that in many ways, they are different from their parents, siblings, and even their friends. Often they'll feel frightened or depressed when this happens, but what they're really feeling is simply the pain of loneliness. Existential loneliness stays with us through life and periodically comes to the surface. Social psychologist Robert Weiss talks about two other types of loneliness: social and emotional. Social loneliness is what people feel when they move to a new community or have very few friends or no real purpose in life. This kind of loneliness can be diminished by taking active strides to create a community for themselves (i.e. joining a church or synagogue, forming a group, or volunteering one's time). By the way, social loneliness gets activated in many people during the holidays when it feels as though the rest of the world is going in a direction different from yours. Often, when people feel they are not like everybody else, the shame makes them feel defective. When emotional loneliness comes from longing for an intimate relationship, it is very painful and more difficult to resolve. Even being married or involved in an intimate relationship doesn't protect us from this kind of loneliness.

Resolving the pain of emotional loneliness is more difficult because it involves another person (and we know how little control we have over others!). I spoke with Psychotherapist Sylvia Elias, who runs groups for single women in Philadelphia titled "One is a Whole Number." I asked her to describe major concerns of the women she worked with over the years. "Most of the women worry about their economics, health, or careers," she said. "Many also worry about who will care for them as they age, but the theme that seems to underlie all of these issues is loneliness and longing for an intimate connection."

I know that some women find solutions more easily than others and seem to be less affected. I wondered what the difference was between these groups. "I think part of the answer is that, for a variety of reasons, some people are just more resilient than others. Some are less affected by loss or other insults to the psyche. Research seems to be pointing toward a brain chemical called seratonin. The new antidepressants such as Prozac, Zoloft, or Paxil are sometimes helpful for this," Elias said. "In addition, the women who are more successful tend to have more purpose in life; they have a reason to get out of bed in the morning; and they have people, activities, or even pets who need them. In addition, people who do better with being alone have what I call an 'internal landscape.' That is a community of family or friends whom they trust and whom they believe think about them when they're not there."

Elias went on to explain that one of her patients recently told her that once she believed in her heart that there were several people who missed her when she was gone, she felt more a part of the world. I told her of my experience that when people talk about their deepest feelings, even the dark ones, with someone who cares, they feel intimate just because they opened up. "That's what the group is really all about. When people have the courage to say 'I'm in pain' or 'I feel lonely,' the loneliness of the moment diminishes," she said.

Writing this column, my thoughts drifted to how lonely life can sometimes be. I then began to think about my own life and how isolated and lonely I sometimes feel. While my mind wandered in this sad reverie, the phone rang. It was a patient rescuing me from a painful situation. I sometimes wonder if am I cursed with my loneliness or blessed with a career that nurtures and sometimes rescues me. I think the answer is yes! What do you think Sarah?

Talking About Pain Helps Overcome It

Dear Dr. Gottlieb,

Two years ago, I was diagnosed with diabetes. My case has been mild, and I have not been very ill. I am 38 years old and have two children ages 12 and 9. My husband is very supportive, but he is not a good listener or communicator.

On one of your shows, you said something like "What a gift it is to be able to share your pain." You were speaking to a daughter about sharing her feelings with her mother. Is it always a good thing to share feelings? My parents never did. I want a better relationship with them; to let go of resentments and make peace with them. I have a lot of hurt inside because I feel nothing I ever did was good enough in their eyes. They didn't have much self-esteem so how could they give what they didn't have?

How can a person with pain open up and be close with the source of that pain? Should I or shouldn't I talk with my parents? I don't want to make a bigger rift.

Suzanne

Dear Suzanne,

When I first read your letter, I wondered why you were telling me about your diabetes and your husband. These issues didn't seem to fit with the rest of your letter. But, knowing the way our minds work, I found a connection.

I remembered back to the years following my accident (I have been a quadriplegic for 13 years). Boy, did I need to talk! I felt like I was bursting inside. I had to tell other people what I was feeling and experiencing in order to make sure I was alive and connected.

Your husband's style may have worked until two years ago (when you were diagnosed), but it sounds like you need more now. Perhaps you need different relationships with your husband, your parents, and maybe even your children.

Since most of your pain centers around your parents, let's start there. You asked if it's good to share feelings. Well, I can emphatically say that not sharing them usually causes harm; it creates a feeling of isolation. So let's see how we can begin to build some bridges in these painful relationships.

Sometimes it's easier to make peace with someone when you understand them. Perhaps you could start by asking your parents about how they feel about themselves; are they as unhappy with themselves as they seem to be with you. If so, ask them why. What baggage do they carry?

After this meeting, if you feel safe enough (safety is a critical ingredient in these discussions), tell them you would like to share some of your feelings with them and ask if they would like to listen—just listen. If they feel blamed or responsible to "fix" something, they may feel defensive and have difficulty really hearing you.

Now comes the hard part. You have to think about what you want them to hear. It wouldn't be helpful to "beat them up" for past hurts but that doesn't mean you shouldn't share your injuries with them. Talk about "your" hurts; not "their" behavior. I would encourage you to tell them what you really want from this relationship; knowing that it can never be ideal for either you or your parents.

Please do your best to tell all of them what's in your heart: the pain, fears, hopes, and wishes. For example, you might want to tell them what it's like to have diabetes. Is it frightening? Do you resent it? Do you wonder if it will shorten your life? What does illness mean to you? The answers to these questions are part of the essence of who you are.

Sharing that information is sharing yourself. It is risky and exciting. Several months ago, my daughter and I went to an Eric Clapton concert at the Spectrum. The house was filled with children and adults singing and dancing to his music. After a while, the lights went down and Clapton sang "Tears in Heaven," a song he sings to his young child who died several years ago. I watched as 17,000 people linked arms and passed tissues. We felt very close to each other. When I thought about it later, I realized that the closeness was generated by just one man sharing his pain, not complaining or feeling sorry for himself, just opening his heart.

Pressing for Unrealistic Goals Can Lead To Lives Of Sadness

"I think I'm just about ready to end therapy now; there's just one remaining problem I need to work on." The patient was a 60 year-old woman with a long history of intermittent depression. She came for help in coping with the variety of changes that had taken place in her life; her daughter had given birth to her first grandchild and her husband just retired. She had done quite well in therapy and was feeling better than she ever had in her life. Although she was delightful to be with, and I enjoyed working with her, I concurred that she was ready to end.

"What's the problem," I asked; "What's left to work on?" "It's these damn ten pounds," she said. "I've been chasing these ten pounds around for the last 40 years; I finally feel self-confident enough so that I really think I have a chance to win this battle." "What's the battle really about?" I asked, knowing that 95 percent of all diets fail anyway. "I always felt that if I could lose these ten pounds, I'd finally feel good about myself and my body."

I left that session feeling quite sad; after all, here was a woman who was successful by most standards. She was content with her 35-year-old marriage which had produced two young adults who were happy with their lives. She was a well-respected professional. She was also quite attractive both in terms of her looks and her personality. Yet she carried the burden of unhappiness that went with those ten pounds for 40 years. How does this happen?

The Industrial Revolution created many wonderful things. It has, in my opinion, also interfered with the growth of the human psyche. Over the centuries, we slowly changed. We gradually learned that we were able to defy gravity, move mountains, and create incredible technology. With all of this newfound power, we stopped looking to nature for guidance and happiness because we assumed we controlled nature. We see this change of direction every day. When we think of what makes us proud or happy, we think in terms of bigger houses, more powerful jobs, better bodies, prettier faces, or successful children. Look at any magazine and you'll see the promises of all of the advertisements: lose weight, cure constipation, perform better, make more money, etc. The problem is that when these efforts fail, and they usually do, we feel as though we've failed. We feel that we should be able to control our bodies and feel ashamed when we don't. Nevertheless, we hold onto the myth that, if we succeed, then we'll find happiness.

Because we spend so much of our time and energy looking outside, we often forget who is inside. The quiet voice that may be saying, "I'm really more comfortable at 140 pounds than I am at 130," gets drowned out next to the music in the aerobics class or the noise at the mall.

When I was in third grade, my teacher had us move up when we got the lesson right and move back when we got our lesson wrong. At the end of the year, I found myself in the last seat, second row—about the 60th percentile. I remember promising myself, "If only I had one more week, I could be the second or third seat in the front row."

I held onto this promise for many years. When I got my first job, it wasn't enough that I was good; I had to be the best. It wasn't enough that I was the best; I had to get an additional part-time job. I was holding on to this promise of the eight year-old boy. By the time I was 28, I had developed a good reputation and a spastic colon.

The evening I learned about my spastic colon, I recall being terribly upset about the implications of such a diagnosis. The doctor told me it was stress-related, and I had to change my lifestyle. "My G-d," I thought, "Here I am, only 28 years old, and I'm already hurting my body with my lifestyle!" I sat alone that evening feeling fear and despair. For some reason, I thought back to the third grade and wondered, for the first time, if I really belonged in the last seat in the second row. "After all," I said to myself, "The kids back there are more like me; and to be honest, I'm really more comfortable there." I almost wept with relief at this realization, and I've been happier ever since.

Tom Fogerty, a family therapist in New Rochelle, New York, often says, "The world is full of people trying to be filet mignon when deep down we know we're only meatballs!"

So, to all my fellow meatballs, stop chasing those ten pounds, or front-row seats, or any other form of perfection. When we give up these relentless and unrealistic demands we place on ourselves, and our loved ones, exciting things can begin to happen. The definition of happiness changes to something with more depth and more access.

Chapter 5...Coping with Loss

What A Parent With Cancer Can Tell A Child

I've been asked by several people to address the issue of what to tell children when their parents are diagnosed with cancer. This is a difficult and important topic with no specific rules. There are, however, some general ways of thinking about the subject that may be helpful.

Children need truth, honesty, and protection. Sometimes these responsibilities are in conflict. When a parent is diagnosed with cancer, the first thing that must be understood is what that diagnosis means to the parents. For some of us a diagnosis of cancer might mean a temporary interruption in our lives and, for some, a death sentence. A diagnosis of cancer might mean loss of a breast, or it might mean loss of a marriage. It is important for parents to understand their own thoughts and emotions about their illness because those emotions will get communicated to their children along with the words. You see, our children are very skilled at hearing their parents' unspoken feelings. After all, their lives depend on this knowledge.

For example, if a parent is terrified yet tells the child that everything is okay, that child will hear the words and feel the terror. To hear one reality and experience another is very confusing and frightening for any of us but worse for a child. If, on the other hand, a parent is terrified and can communicate to a child, "Yes, I'm scared; but we'll go through it together," the child will understand a bit more of his/her own painful reality.

When a parent is diagnosed with cancer, this introduces psychic pain to the family system. It cannot be avoided, denied, or minimized. It is, in

122

fact, a tragic reality that a young child must learn about these things at a young age. It is a parent's instinct to protect a child from pain. However, we cannot protect our children by denying reality, especially when it communicates these "truths" to our children.

Much of the answer involves the child's age. Young children, of course, need more protection than older children. Very young children need to know that their basic needs will be taken care of. They generally aren't that interested in the illness or what it may mean in the long run. Older children generally want more information. Many parents are confused as to how much information to share. As a rule of thumb, it's always helpful to allow children to ask whatever questions they like; and we should answer them as fully as possible.

Keep in mind that children sometimes ask very incisive and painful questions. They may ask, "Are you going to die? What does it mean to die? Who will take care of me after you're gone?" These questions should not be glossed over but need to be dealt with directly. It's unfair to say to children, "You shouldn't think or feel that; it won't happen," as it minimizes or denies their fears and their reality. Usually, when we do this to our children, it serves to allay our anxiety more than theirs.

Also, it is not safe to assume that older children will do better than younger ones. Research suggests that adolescents may have a difficult time with a parent's serious illness. They may become depressed, withdrawn or angry, or suffer a variety of other symptoms. After all, a teenager's main job is to grow to early adulthood and leave the nest. A serious illness certainly interferes with that process.

The main task we have when we talk to our children about cancer or any serious illness is to listen. Our children need time, space, and emotional safety to talk about their feelings and what their parent's illness means to them. Listening sounds easy enough; but in order to truly hear the experience of another, the waters in our souls must be quiescent. Children, ideally, should be able to experience a parent as calm enough to contain their worst nightmares; to really listen without getting upset or trying to silence their fears. This is not realistic. After all, you've just been traumatized too. The waters inside are probably anything but calm, and this kind of turmoil generally interferes with our ability to listen.

Please be patient with yourself and your family. This is a painful and difficult process. I encourage you to share some of your fears with your family. It may give them an opportunity to do something for you by listening and supporting you through your difficult times. This may also help them to open their hearts to you. I believe that almost all crises also present us with an opportunity—an opportunity for increased appreciation and respect for each other, ourselves, and life itself.

I recently asked a man who had cancer several years ago if it had changed his life. He said, "I hope so—I hope I never forget what I learned from the experience."

In Bill Moyers' book *Healing and the Mind*, there is a poem written by a woman who had terminal cancer. I believe it explains what is possible:

> Don't talk about your troubles.
> No one loves a sad face.
> Oh, Mom, the truth is
> cheer isolates,
> humor defends,
> competence intimidates,
> control separates,
> and sadness,
> sadness opens us up to each other.

Reflecting On Life Can Be The Best Way For Family To Cope With Death

Dear Dr. Gottlieb:

My husband of 30 years has been battling cancer for the last eight months. Last week he told me he has "no more fight left" in him. I'll never forget those sad eyes. This man has been my partner and my strength for almost 30 years, and now I don't know what to do.

How can I help Eric be more comfortable? How can I help our three children, who range from 19 to 28 years old, cope with the loss of their father? Most of all, what am I to do with me? How can I live with the terrible guilt about what I should do? Should I continue the battle that he can't? If I do, he gets ravished with more treatments. If I don't…

I've got all of this fear and anger. I even envy my friends. The only one who would understand me is my husband. What's the right thing to do?

Carol

Dear Carol:

I'm sorry for what you and your family are about to lose and what you've lost already. Understand that there are no rights and wrongs here; the five of you have to cope with the terrible injustice of this death the best you can. The pain is inevitable; it's the price we pay for love.

The sad fact is that dying is a lonely process. Very few people can really understand what it's like to face their own death. On the other hand, for you and your children, losing a best friend and a father is equally lonely. This is not the time to protect one another from your grief, anger, and fear. Protecting our loves ones only creates barriers and makes everyone even more lonely and isolated. Although death can be a lonely process, it can also be a very intimate one. As difficult as this may sound, I recommend your family begin to reflect on your lives together.

Recently, I saw, in consultation, a family in which the mother was terminally ill. She, her husband, and adult children talked about what were the most important parts of their history. Despite having traveled the world, her fondest memories were in the very small moments in life; dinner with her family, watching television with her husband, and sending her daughters off to school when they were young.

Her statement helped everyone in the room understand that what is most important in life is lived in the small amounts. From that statement, we all learned more about life than we did about death.

Ask Eric to talk about his life; his regrets and joys, and you to do the same. Also, if you haven't done so already, it is important for all five of you to share your beliefs about what happens after death. His body may be dying, but his mind and spirit may be very alive. In many respects, he can continue to be your strength.

I treasure the time I spent with my sister two years ago as she was dying from a rapidly growing brain tumor. I taped our talks as she told me about what her life and death meant to her. I was touched when she told me how much she had enjoyed and appreciated her life. And although she was sad and angry that it was ending, she had no regrets. And, when she listened to me as I told her about my grief, fear, and outrage, it felt like she was still my big sister helping me with something painful. I could almost see when she crossed the threshold from fear of death to being at peace with it; that helped me more than anything else.

As far as your guilt is concerned, I think almost anyone in your position would feel guilty. That's because we sometimes use guilt to protect us from deeper pain such as loss or the feelings of helplessness. However, it's important to remember that Eric's life and death are in his hands, not yours. As long as his judgment is intact, it's his call. Despite my words, Eric is the only one who can really help you and your guilt. Please talk to him about it. His reassurance could be very healing for you.

When people feel as overwhelmed as you are, what they secretly wish for is someone to take care of them and work out all these problems.

Although nobody can resolve the problems for you, a good hospice can help. Hospice services can include visiting nurses and doctors to help your husband be more comfortable and take some of the burden off you. They also provide social workers and grief counselors who will be able to help you and your family cope with many of these difficult issues both now and after Eric's death.

Their Life Was Filled With Love, But Then The Husband Died In Anger

Dear Dr. Gottlieb:

I just lost my 50 year-old husband after a three-month illness. Ed was told, two months before he died, that he should put his affairs in order. He did. Many of our family and many of our friends came to call; his last months seemed like one big love feast showered on both of us. He said his last goodbyes to loved ones and told them what they meant to him; what a gift!

Before the illness, we had a wonderful relationship filled with love and laughter. After coming through two particularly poor first marriages, we found each other. We had the usual stepfamily issues in the beginning, but we decided we would work them out no matter what. Ed was proud of my successes in the business world and tremendously supportive of anything I tried to do.

In short, after years of struggle, we found a way of life that worked for us. We even noticed family and friends were drawn to our company. Ed never let anyone treat me with anything but respect, and he did the same.

My problem—during his last month, while treating everyone with the utmost respect, he treated me as someone he hardly knew. He bossed me around, leaned on me constantly, and generally was not the person I knew. He spoke so disrespectfully to me that, at times, I was brought to tears.

I'm trying to tell myself he probably knew I was going to survive and he wouldn't, and he was angry about that. But, I'm tormented by his treatment. Why couldn't we have ended our time together lovingly?

Tormented

Dear Tormented:

I was sorry about your tragic loss. You're right to assume Ed was angry and had no good way to express it. What happened to you both was an outrageous assault on your happy lives, and it's common to feel rage, shock, and disbelief. After all, life as you've known it was about to be torn from you. What can one do with all these confusing, painful, and uncomfortable emotions?

Shortly after an accident 15 years ago that left me a quadriplegic, my ex-wife came to visit me at the hospital during physical therapy one day. As part of the exercise, the therapist asked us to tap a beach ball to each other so I could relearn my balancing skills. After about 15 seconds, we were hitting the ball at each other a little harder than necessary. Nervous and confused, we continued for several minutes. By the end, we were slamming the ball at one another with our teeth bared!

As we talked about it later, we realized that during the exercise we were both furious and had no way to express it. I shudder to think what we would have done to each other without the ball! I believe we both felt betrayed by one another. After all, we promised (as unrealistic as it may be) to take care of one another. Through no fault of our own, we both reneged on that promise, and we were furious. The same happened with you and Ed; you were both betrayed by his illness.

You said you were "Tormented," but it's helpful to understand what that means to you and why you're feeling that way. Tormented might mean frightened, angry, confused, outraged, or abandoned. Are you tormented because he left you the way he did? Are you tormented because you're angry with him for his disrespect? Are you tormented because he left you alone to deal with what might be the most painful time of your life? As hurtful as it may have been, Ed apparently was able to express his outrage to you, but what about your feelings? Did you ever tell Ed you were angry or scared that he was leaving you? Your inability to express these emotions may be contributing to your torment.

I spoke with Sharon Carr, grief counselor at the Hospice of the Delaware Valley. She feels all relationships must end "properly." "The way he died robbed her of the ability to say goodbye in a manner that fit the dignity and affection of their relationship. All relationships have a beginning, middle, and end. If it's not ended properly, there's no good way to grieve the loss and the pain lingers."

For healing to begin, what you're feeling inside must have a voice and must be expressed. Carr finds rituals can be helpful: "Creating a ritual way of saying goodbye often helps make the experience more real. The ritual should include conversation with the deceased in which feelings can be expressed and statements can be made. The ritual can be done either alone or in the presence of loved ones who can witness the event. I often recommend the 'empty-chair technique' in which the person in mourning imagines the loved one sitting in an empty chair across from her. The environment must be safe enough so she can ask anything, say anything, or even explode with emotion if she needs to. It often is done with a therapist who is familiar with the technique. It can also be done simply by writing a letter if that fits the person's style. It's also important to remember that grief is a long process. A ritual may need to be repeated several times. It's not unusual for someone in mourning to still feel pain three to five years after the death."

The other important ingredient in healing is forgiveness. We must ultimately forgive our loved ones for leaving us, and we must forgive ourselves for what we did or didn't do before they died.

I believe most things in life have a purpose. Painful as it is, perhaps your torment is a way of keeping you connected to Ed for the moment. Many theologians, philosophers, and spiritual leaders will agree that death also has a purpose. At the very least, death helps us understand how fragile and precious life is. In order to dignify the life and death of those we've lost, I believe we must learn that lesson.

Exploring The Anxiety About Death And Loss

Dr. Gottlieb:

I'm finding that as I age (I'm 50 now), I begin to get more and more concerned about death; not my death, but deaths of members of my family who are older. My parents are in their 70s; and despite their relatively good health, I think about their deaths all the time. Even worse, my brother and sister are only a few years older than me, and I have become consumed by thoughts and fears about their deaths.

It has gotten to a point where I feel depressed, anxious, and burdened by all of these worries. I really hate living with all of this anxiety. Is it time to seek professional help? Is there any medication out that could take away the pain and help me to return to the woman I once was?

Joan

Dear Joan:

In general, I advise people to seek treatment when whatever is going on inside them emotionally begins to interfere with their lives. If your concern about death has begun to interfere with your ability to sleep, work, eat, relate to loved ones, or enjoy your life, I would recommend treatment.

Your question about medication is a bit more complicated. I'm not a physician and, therefore, cannot give medication advice. But, there are some medications on the market that have been demonstrated to be helpful with the kind of "obsessive thinking" that you seem to be suffering. In addition, it is well known that there are more effective antidepressants on the market than ever before.

Research being done on the biology of emotion has shown that certain medication can be helpful with your type of problem. Both Peter Kramer who wrote *Listening to Prozac* and Donald Nathanson who wrote *Shame and Pride* talk about biochemical changes in the brain that are the underpinnings of emotion. As a result of this research, the pharmaceutical industry is generating drugs that are more and more elegant and effective. Therefore, I would recommend that you consult with a competent psychiatrist or psychopharmacologist about medication.

However, there is more to the life and story of Joan than a simple pill or two or a series of neuro-chemical connections in the brain. Your thoughts about death may have to do with many things related to you as a person and you as an inhabitant of this planet.

Every living being from age 3 or 4 on begins to understand and fear death. We struggle with it in a thousand different ways throughout our life cycle. When we are adolescents, we turn our back on death and deny its existence. When we reach middle age and realize we can't avoid it, many get obsessive about their diet and exercise. Some get depressed and frightened. These struggles have to do with being alive and realizing your life is more than half over.

If you could take a pill that would wipe out those concerns (I don't believe there is one yet), it would make you a little bit less human; a little bit less Joan. As part of your treatment, I hope you begin to understand what death means to you and to explore the pain and angst of saying goodbye to your parents and siblings; do it slowly and carefully. To engage in that process (ideally with a good therapist) is to learn more about Joan, to bring more of Joan to the surface, and make her more alive. Isn't it funny how dealing with death can ultimately make us more alive? I believe that's the only way to do it.

By the way, one of your requests was to return to being the woman you once were. Well, fortunately or unfortunately, you can't. You never were a 50 year-old woman who has faced death in the way you're facing it now. You know things you never really knew before. You can be happier and less obsessed than you are now, but you can never be who you once were; none of us can.

As an aside, I'm concerned about a controversy that has developed among mental health professionals. It seems that one camp has focused its work on the brain. These adherents are making some exciting new discoveries about brain chemistry, genetics, and their relationship to mood and emotion.

Some think that medical and chemical manipulation could go a long way toward diminishing not just major psychiatric problems such as depression, schizophrenia, and manic-depression; but also many of the personal and social ills we live with, including hyper-sensitivity, irritability, and milder depressions. I find the work both exciting and frightening. To treat the body and ignore the soul is dangerous. On the other hand, to only treat the mind and ignore these important discoveries can result in subjecting patients and their families to unnecessary suffering. Carl Jung said that psychic pain comes from the avoidance of "legitimate suffering." Sometimes, however, medication can help someone avoid legitimate work that needs to be done in order that we can know our demons and ourselves.

I was recently asked the difference between body and soul. My answer was there is no difference. I believe a piece of our soul can be found in every cell in our body. To think that we can work with the soul, spirit, psyche and not address ourselves at the cellular level is to deny a very important part of ourselves. To try to manage the cells and not acknowledge that what we are really managing is the soul of another person can be terribly dangerous and injurious.

As I say to both partners in a marriage, please listen to each other; allow this relationship to grow based on mutual respect and dignity. If this relationship ends up in divorce, we're all in trouble!

Anniversary Of A Loss Can Be A Painful Time

The holidays are happy times. Christmas is a birthday; Chanukah is a festival of lights, and Kwanzaa is a new beginning.

Because everyone is supposed to be happy during that time of year, people who aren't can feel pretty alienated. Take my friends Ron and Kathy, whose 16-year old daughter died of leukemia seven years ago on December 18 or all of the other parents who lost children around the holidays. The anniversary of a death is always a difficult time, especially that of a child. But many people feel ashamed or guilty for experiencing sadness in the face of a joyous world around them. I've heard many people say, "After all these years, I shouldn't be in this much pain."

The fact is an anniversary of a loss always reminds us of whom or what we've lost. Ron and Kathy devote the day to talking about their daughter. They think about her smile and magnetic personality. "It feels painful and good at the same time," Ron said recently. "We used to just think of her (as she was) during the last few months when she was so sick; now we're starting to remember the good times, too." "The holiday season makes the mourning more difficult," he said, because he and Kathy feel even more alone with their pain. "Loss of a child is a nightmare, and naturally people tend to shy away. I guess the holidays just give them a better excuse. I understand."

People in mourning need compassion. Compassion can diminish the sense of alienation. But what goes on inside the hearts and minds of someone who has lost a child around the holidays? I've often heard the phrase, "When a parent dies, you lose a past; when a child dies, you lose a future."

In addition to the anguish, many who have lost a child describe terrible and often life-long guilt. Some call it survivors' guilt. "My child shouldn't have died, I should have," or "If only I hadn't let him use the car that night," are typical voices of survivors' guilt. In a way, guilt is a way to find meaning in the chaos of a child's death. If we can affix blame, the loss can be explained.

Many parents feel that the pain is a way of staying loyal to their child. When the pain diminishes, they fear the memory will also; that's not true. It is also very common for people mourning the death of a child to feel angry, even furious. After all, they've had their future stolen and any theft makes us angry.

Death of a child can be especially difficult for siblings, even if they are born after the death. Often, a deceased child is deified, thus making it impossible for other children to establish their own identities. They also may not feel entitled to ask questions or express their grief for fear of hurting their parents. On the other hand, some parents will try to deny their anguish by not talking about it. They do this partly because of the pain and partly to "protect" the other children. Of course, this approach rarely works—the unexpressed pain just gets felt by everyone.

The pain of unresolved grief can have a devastating impact. Some have estimated that the divorce rate is 80 percent when a child dies. And the effects can last beyond one generation. For example, if children grow up in an environment where the pain is silent, it could affect whom, or if, they marry and how they raise their own children.

All of these issues are reactivated around an anniversary. In order to get through these difficult times, it may be helpful for bereaved families to remember several things:

- The pain you feel is normal and natural. Although the anguish may not last forever, the grief and sadness may last a lifetime.
- This day is an opportunity to talk with your loved ones. Don't be afraid to discuss your feelings. Probably everybody in the family feels

something similar. Talk may or may not diminish the pain, but it certainly will help everyone feel less alone.

- Many people use this day to revisit the memory and spirit of their child or sibling. They do it through visiting a gravesite, praying, or writing a letter.
- Remember, the goal is not to diminish the pain—that can't be done anyway. Don't try to manipulate your thoughts or feelings; it's unnatural and disrespectful.
- Compassion and empathy can diminish the loneliness that goes with mourning. Try to surround yourself with people who are willing to understand who and what you've lost.

To friends of bereaved families: As caring people, our impulse is to try to diminish the pain of people we care about. That usually does more harm than good. The message we give them when that happens is, "You shouldn't feel what you feel." If they're depressed, that will make them more depressed. If they're not depressed, it might just make them angry. They don't need your encouragement or sympathy, just your caring. Ask questions like: "How are you today? What do you think about?" Or, "I know how much you loved her. What is it like several years after her death?"

People in mourning don't need answers or advice. They need questions and companionship from people who can tolerate their pain.

Coping When Illness Hits A Family Member

My mother called two months ago to tell me "Dan, your sister has a headache; she's had it all week." I felt mildly burdened and annoyed by this information I didn't want and so I quickly buried it. Several days later my mother called again and said, "She's still got a headache." I was becoming frightened against my will.

The next week my mother called with yet another report, sounding even more urgent; "Now she's having trouble reading." Fear and dread began to set in and yet I told myself, "It's Sharon; she's strong; not her." But, I wanted to hear it from the doctor. I could feel a very dark cloud beginning to form in my life.

A week later we discovered she had "what appeared to be a tumor." I felt assaulted, panicked, and angry. Then came fear and further denial. "It can't be, I said to myself." I clung to the assessment of one doctor who said reassuringly, "I'm sure it's benign; it's nothing to worry about it."

Surgery took place a couple of weeks later, and the family waited in the hospital all day. We survived it with gallows humor and gin rummy; still hoping that it was "nothing." When the surgeon informed us at 5 p.m. that it was "something," the news was too frightening to feel. Through my tears, I saw my brother-in-law and nephews respond as though they'd just been beaten.

Since that day, we've been hearing about radiation, chemotherapy, "promising research," and never-ending probability statements. Feeling as if I had entered a dark tunnel, I called my friend and colleague John Valentine, a psychiatrist who specializes in the boundary between physical illness and emotions. Despite my personal history with illness, my head felt devoid of knowledge and understanding. Needing some guideposts, I asked him to describe what goes on in families when they go through this kind of nightmare. Here's what he said: "The hardest thing for families to talk about is life itself; how shaky it is, how vulnerable and precious, how unfair, how arbitrary. They learn the negative side of life can be very big anyway you look at it.

"The people on their case become magicians, capable of miracles. And, yet they can't turn back the clock, despite the wish… They often feel the whole system stinks and disability or worse is there at the end. They may wonder, 'Is it worth it for us to agree with the hospital, this modern equivalent of a Gothic cathedral and its grounds?' What alternative do we have?"

My friend recalled a patient he had years ago named Lisa. She was 35 when she went home with a diagnosis of multiple myeloma; a type of blood cancer. "There was a hole in the family where the normal Lisa used to be, even as little as two weeks earlier, when the paleness and weakness and back pain put her in the hospital. She may live another 50 years, but she will never be a non-patient to her clan. There may always be a special thought or a special mental pause as they speak to or about Lisa. They are not 'living with illness' yet; it is too soon. It takes six to 12 months for the family to digest what is illness and what are ordinary aches and pains. Then it was all in that black hole called Lisa's sickness.

"But despite the shock and pain, early healing of the family wound had begun to occur at the edges. In teeniest details and cosmic upliftings, the human spirit began its repair work. Relatives prayed and Lisa, still feeling unreal, had flickers of critical questions like, 'What is life all about? What does mine mean to me and what do I want to do with it?' To ask questions like that of one's self is to begin to face and conquer our darkest fears. These are thoughts and feelings both patients and families have whether or not they talk about them."

Sick children, Valentine says, will often want what he calls an environmental impact statement about their lives ahead. They want to know, "How different from other kids will I have to be?"

Valentine noted that every parent's worse nightmare is the thought of having to bury a child. And it isn't any easier when it's an adult child. During a serious illness parents may wonder, "How can I be of real help when I am failing myself?"

He says other relatives may wonder whether they can really level with the patient about their feelings, such as "How much life will the future hold and for how long?" Practical thoughts often creep in here about work, benefits, changing the house, other medication. Spouses may privately think, "How will I and our marriage get through this?" The couple is low, they are battered, false hope is gone, a solid bottom to push off from has not yet reached, and everybody is sick of sickness.

As the family's campaign against the illness begins, they all need to conduct themselves so that win, lose, or draw, they can all sleep at night knowing that they conducted themselves with honor and grace in their time of trouble. Some fight, some follow the rules, some just stay steady on... Gothic cathedrals and modern hospitals are shacks compared to the mysterious depths of families. So the clans gather around the sick one. They did it 50,000 years ago in caves. It's our social instinct. It's the social contract. It's health insurance you can't legislate. It's three or 23 minds working on a problem personal to them all. All will be givers and takers, players and on-lookers, pushers and opposers, heroes and villains; sometimes in the same person at different times. It is humans at their most human and the hand of G-d in action.

To be traumatized by news like this can leave you feeling very, very alone, yet closer to family and closer to life itself. When I left my friends and colleagues to go to the hospital that day, I was one kind of Dan. After we got the news, I felt as if I was different. I could tell my story, but they couldn't "really" understand. My family could.

When I saw my sister sick for the first time, I loved her in a way I never did before.

Getting Past Fear Of Change By Accepting The Loss Of A Loved One

I always loved Sharon. I looked up to her as my older sister. She was a role model I both idolized and envied. Of course we fought often as children; but as we matured, so did our relationship. With marriage, children, and the crises of life our relationship grew deeper and more intimate.

When she was first diagnosed with brain cancer, the change in her was almost imperceptible; but I could see that the gleam in her eye was gone.

She just wasn't the old Sharon anymore. I was scared. Who is she now I wondered? Is this the beginning of the end? I felt terribly hurt and bereaved that she was just a half step slower than she had been; just a drop less focused. The loss looked small, but I really felt it. Within a couple of weeks, I realized that not only was I tolerating the change, but also now I loved this Sharon, the new one.

Over time, she became more aphasic; had trouble finding words to express her thoughts and feelings—frustrating for both of us. I felt fear and grief, and then I loved her again.

Six months later, I went to visit her and her husband, David, in Florida while she was recuperating from her second brain surgery. This Sharon was radically different. She couldn't remember about 30 percent of her words. Her gait was unsteady. She was more confused; I had to help her dial the telephone and use the correct utensils at meals. For the first day and a half of my five-day visit, I was absolutely traumatized. During the week, we went to the movies and dinners, and the three of us talked for many hours. By the end of the week, my affection and admiration for her was renewed, and I couldn't wait to see her again.

Last month, she began to slip into a coma. When I visited her at home, she was fairly unresponsive. As I held her hand and cried while I said my final goodbyes, I saw her eyes well up with tears also. After 20 or 30 minutes, I ran out of things to say. The silence was uncomfortable, but I didn't want to leave her room. I cried for a long time before I left but came back an hour later because I missed her. You see, I even loved the Sharon who was in a coma.

All loss is change. All change is loss. That's why we fight so hard to resist change. Change, even for the better, is a loss for us. That's why some people feel sad even after a good thing happens like a job promotion or moving to a nicer home. We've all known people who had been hurt by something that happened in the past and never seemed to get beyond it. That's because many of us would rather hold on to yesterday's pain than face an unknown tomorrow. A parent's aging, a child's sadness, or newly

eness all represents change for us and, therefore, loss.
eason we get so angry when a loved one changes.

stinct to resist change rather than to mourn the loss it
represc.. time I saw Sharon in a different state, I wanted to scream: "Please don't leave me!" I didn't think I could tolerate the pain and loneliness I felt with each of her changes. Perhaps we all feel something similar when someone or something important to us changes. These changes represent small deaths. Perhaps what dies is a dream; perhaps what dies is part of the illusion that we have control of our lives. Regardless of what dies, each death must be mourned if we are to reclaim our lives.

Social scientist and author Stephen Levine describes grief as the "The rope burns left behind when something we dearly loved has been pulled from our grasp against our will." The pain of losing something precious can be excruciating. This pain should not be avoided, denied, or blamed on someone else. When we experience death, whether it's a small symbolic one like the loss of lifestyle or the death of a loved one, we suffer. Suffering, like death, cannot be avoided.

While Sharon was dying, I couldn't pretend I wasn't feeling loss. There was no illusion that she would be like she was. As she was leaving, maybe because she was leaving, I loved her even more. How tragic that we sometimes forget that the people we love will someday die.

"Death is not the greatest loss in life. The greatest loss is what dies inside us while we live." Norman Cousins.

Sad News

I have previously written a column about a woman who was frustrated with her husband because he apparently did not say no to others' requests.

It was a second marriage for both and the writer said that, by and large, the marriage was good, but she was frustrated. I recently received the following letter:

Dear Dr. Gottlieb:

Much has happened to us since that article. My husband is quite ill following radiation treatments for cancer. It left him with internal bleeding. Now I am writing you because of your personal experiences with loss.

Dear Reader:

I'm terribly sorry for what you both are going through. I'm sure your mutual love and devotion will help you get through this together. The simple answer to your question about how we live with adversity is this: We live with it because we are humans, and that's what we do. It is our instinct to go on—to live. Of course, the situation is not simple; nor are the emotions both of you are experiencing. Cancer is a life-altering diagnosis. From the moment we hear that word, life will never be the same again. Feelings of terror, grief, anger, sadness, and helplessness may well come and go from moment to moment. And most who have battled cancer will tell you that this process can also bring clarity and a new perspective on what is precious and what is unimportant.

Several years ago, as my sister's condition was deteriorating from brain cancer, I went for a visit. No one else was in the house, so she offered to make me a cup of tea. Because her condition was worsening, she had a great deal of difficulty with the process. Because I could not reach the cabinets from my wheelchair, I talked her through the process that took about 20 minutes. When she finally put the cup in front of me, we looked at each other and smiled. I can still remember the taste of that tea. I wish for you and your husband many precious moments.

Painful Lessons Learned About Love, Death And Life—All From A Cat

Several years ago I wrote a column about a 16 year-old cat named Gary. At the time, my daughter Alison was a college student working in a veterinary hospital. Gary was a street cat that had been dropped off at that hospital several months earlier. The staff tried to adopt him, as its mascot, but couldn't because of his various medical problems. He had a heart murmur, only one tooth, and a bad attitude; despite being on Valium, he would urinate wherever and whenever he felt like it. Alison couldn't stand to see him put to sleep, so she took him home.

Alison devoted several weeks to taking care of him. She withdrew all medication, kept him in her room and read to him, watched television with him, and slept with him. Slowly, he developed into an obedient, devoted, and loving cat. It was almost as though he knew she saved his life and loved him despite all of his problems.

Last week, Gary died. He had developed an illness over the last six months that caused him to deteriorate very slowly. Despite suffering the recent deaths of both her grandmothers and her mother, Alison had never watched death up close. She learned many painful lessons. She discovered that as soon as you realize you will lose someone you love, the relationship becomes more precious than ever. I learned this lesson when a terminal brain tumor was diagnosed in my sister several years ago. And I see it in my cancer support group in the loving and devoted looks husbands give their wives who are battling metastatic breast cancer.

She also learned that passing away is literally that. Almost every day, Ali could see that a little more of Gary was gone. Slowly his heart weakened, then his lungs. His muscles became fatigued, and walking became difficult. The more someone seems to slip away, the tighter we hold on. Toward the end, Alison would never leave Gary's side. She took him to work and then stayed home with him evenings and weekends. Just as in the beginning, they were always together. It seemed the closer he came to the end of life, the more she loved him.

But her experience with Gary taught her something about life itself. The Talmud says that every blade of grass has an angel standing over it saying, "Grow, grow." The angel is the life force. She saw it in Gary as he fought with cancer and congestive heart failure, trying to reclaim his life. I see it every day in my patients who abuse drugs and alcohol in a misguided attempt to keep their internal demons at bay so that they, too, can live. I see it in my patients with multiple personality disorders who break up their minds to make the pain bearable so they, too, can live. Or my friend who, upon learning of the reoccurrence of her breast cancer, said: "I don't have the strength to go through this. I just can't do it." And how several sentences later this terrified and depleted woman said: "Do you know a good oncologist I could see?"

The life force. That's what Gary taught Alison.

And Alison learned about the price we pay for love. The deeper the love, the deeper the pain. Writer and lecturer Stephen Levine says, "Grief is the rope burns left behind when what we have clutched so tightly is pulled from our grasp against our will." When Gary died, I spent the following day with Alison. She wept easily and openly with each reminder of his presence—or absence. At the end of the day, she seemed surprised by something. "When I went home," she said, "I was greeted by my two other cats, a dog, and my boyfriend. Nevertheless, the house still seemed empty."

I shared this anonymously written poem titled, "Lost Parts," with her:

> You told me how a friend of yours
> had caught a bad one through the knee,
> and under two days heavy fire
> had spoiled like meat left out too long
> so that they had to take the leg

at the hip, and how he cried
because it hurt, the leg still hurt,
even years after it had gone
to ground, part of the soil it died on,
how he'd scratch itches in the air
without relief. That's how this is,
like Rachel's wailing for her children.
The phantom ache of something gone.

I told Alison that I believed this is the source of all pain. It hurts where
yesterday used to be. The relationship between Gary and Alison was very
special. She saved his life; and in turn, he taught her about love, death,
and life itself. All of this from a 20-year-old cat with one tooth, a heart
murmur, and a rebellious bladder.

Chapter 6... The Evolving Human Spirit

In The Face Of Loss, Celebration Of Human Resilience

There is a biblical commentary that says: "Every blade of grass has an angel standing over it saying, 'Grow, grow.'" I know that the life force is phenomenal, unexplainable, and resilient; I know that from many sources. I know it from the substance abusers I see who consume dangerous chemicals to quiet the demons of a raging brain. I know from the adults who exhibit bizarre or destructive symptoms as an effort to segregate their thoughts and feelings, past and present, just so they can stay one step ahead of an horrific history. And I know about this life force from personal experience.

On December 20, 1979 I kissed my wife and little girls goodbye, walked across my frozen lawn, and climbed into my brown 1976 Ford Mustang. How could I know those few steps on that clear crisp morning were the last I would ever take?

While I was driving on the turnpike several hours later, a tractor-trailer going in the opposite direction lost its rear wheel. The wheel bounced across the turnpike, crushed my car, and severed my spinal cord. From that moment, I could neither move nor feel anything below my chest... In those first several months, I wished only for death and relief from this terrible nightmare. My commitment to the welfare of my young daughters was the only thing that kept me alive from day to day.

In March 1980, I went to Magee Hospital for rehabilitation. At the end of the day, I would sit in my wheelchair looking out of a picture window on Race Street and feel nothing but bitterness and envy toward everyone who walked or drove by. Even the man sleeping on the vent on 16th and Race didn't escape my bitterness, "At least he can get up and walk away if he wants to," I remember thinking. I believed that nothing could be worse than quadriplegia; nothing.

That was 20 years ago. Today, I envy no one. What's the difference between then and now? I am certainly not a hero. Nor am I the kind of guy who makes lemonade out of lemons—it's just not my style!

The difference is the resilience of the human spirit. Certainly a portion of resilience is mysterious, but we also have learned that resilience depends on many factors: social, psychological, environmental, and even genetic. I was fortunate to have had a supportive family, many friends, and a career as a psychologist that allowed me to make a contribution to the world.

Looking back, I realize that my envy of others began to diminish as my "new" life developed. When people first started asking for advice and consultation, I began to realize that I had value. The more fulfillment people experience in their lives, the less likely they are to envy anyone or anything.

Several years later, when I faced even greater adversity and found myself living alone and confined to bed, I rediscovered a spiritual dimension of my life—another important ingredient in resilience. And so the evolution of healing continued. Given an environment of support, respect, and safety, more often than not the human spirit will heal itself.

I have never seen evidence of this as clearly as I did in a couples group I ran for the Linda Creed Breast Cancer Foundation. Over the course of a two-year group, I saw seven couples who were dealing with varying stages of breast cancer.

While the group was together, we went to four funerals and witnessed incredible sadness, love, and courage. I watched as these women and their husbands fought valiantly for life. And then, when somehow they knew that fight was over, each man seemed to cross a threshold and actually see the husbands at the funerals of their beloved wives. Despite knowing this day would come, they looked stunned and bereft, their eyes empty. Then slowly, over the course of weeks, months, and years, the emotional bleeding stopped. Their emotions seemed to go from screaming agony every waking minute to an ache and longing that may last a lifetime. The heart may be broken, but the spirit is resilient.

Over the years, I have learned some other things about the human spirit. My dog usually works with me in my psychotherapy practice and has developed some pretty good instincts. When patients become very upset during a session, he frequently will go to them and lie on his back there. No matter how upset people are, they inevitably wind up rubbing his belly. Sometimes that act alone helps them feel better. I believe it is our instinct to help one another.

Similarly, when I am alone on the street, I rarely worry about getting help if a door needs opening or if I develop a mechanical problem with my wheelchair. People always seem to volunteer. And usually after such an encounter, we both feel better. A study done several years ago demonstrated that the process of helping others actually increased endorphins; neurotransmitters associated with happiness.

The desires to grow and belong are part of what drives us; so are the pursuits of happiness and meaning; and we pursue these things in the face of incredible adversity—that is something for all of us to celebrate this season.

From The Simple Wisdom Of A Dog; Profound Lessons On Life

I have a cocker spaniel named Aldo. We're both middle-aged. I can tell he's getting older because his muzzle is turning gray, and he makes middle-aged noises when he sleeps. Although my muzzle is also gray, it's pretty easy to tell us apart. When we work together in my psychotherapy practice, I'm the one with the glasses doing a lot of nodding and talking.

Aldo doesn't do much when we work except sleep and make those funny noises, but every now and then he intervenes with a brilliant observation. The other day we were in session with a 35 year-old woman who was complaining about her relationships in general and men specifically. "If only I could find a man who wasn't afraid to make a commitment," she said. It seems they're either running away from a relationship; or if they stay, they're so demanding, it feels that I have no room to breathe. Why can't I find a man with enough self-confidence to both love me and allow me to be my own person?"

At that moment, Aldo woke up, jumped off the sofa, and licked her hand, suggesting, "I can do all those things—I'll stay faithful and make very few demands of you." After we laughed, she realized that although her needs sounded simple, people aren't. They are complicated personalities with needs and wishes of their own.

Dogs are simple, and it did get me thinking about what we can learn from a dog's simple perspective. A few months ago, I was in session with a man who was feeling angry, frightened, and sad over the realization that he was more than 50 years old; and his opportunities to realize his dreams were slipping away. He talked about his regrets and his fear of dying. After a while, he began to weep.

As he quietly wept, Aldo woke up with a very confused expression on his face. It was as if he was thinking: "I don't understand all this angst about life and death. It seems to me that you're born, look for food, find somebody to walk you, take a nap, and you die. What's the problem? Boy, you humans are certainly a funny species!"

I wondered if his perspective was simplistic or insightful. There is rich wisdom in "simple" thinking. We have been given the gift of critical thought but like most gifts, if overused, it can become a curse. For example, many of us have turned ruminating and agonizing into an art form! "If my child wears a cotton sweater, she'll be uncomfortable when the sun comes out." "If I wear a red tie to talk to my boss, what will she think of me?" "If, then, what about… "

We sometimes become so consumed with worrying about our lives and doing things the right way that we diminish our opportunity to actually live. After all, time spent worrying is time lived in the head. To be happy, we must spend just as much time in our hearts.

Last summer I took a walk with a 4 year-old friend of mine. When she arrived, I was just completing my fourth project of the day and thinking about how much I still had to do before the sun went down. That day I was very much living in my head. When we started our walk, I asked her what she did that day. "Nuthin," she said. Undaunted, I persisted. "What did you do yesterday?" "Nuthin." She looked a little bored. I asked about three more stupid "grown-up" questions before I realized that this child had no sense of time. While I was discovering this insight, she was discovering an anthill. We looked at this anthill for a long time. We gave some of the ants names and made up stories about what they were doing. At the end of our walk, I felt much better—less worried about things, living in my heart instead of my head.

There is much to be learned in the simple activity of spending the day with a child or watching the "wisdom" of a dog. This activity helps to slow brain activity and put life into perspective. In watching the world around us, we can understand that it has been here for centuries before we got here, and hopefully, will be here for centuries after we're gone and that simple understanding can calm a raging ego that is always demanding more of us and our loved ones.

When people come to my door, Aldo is thrilled to see them. He doesn't have an ego that wonders if that person is prettier or wealthier. He doesn't care if he or she is depressed, happy, old, or young. He doesn't even care if it's another animal (unless it's the boxer next door). He apparently just loves his life and everybody else's.

It seems to me that a lot can be learned in the simple wisdom of Aldo. Perhaps, the saying is true that our teachers come from strange places.

Who would have thought that my current teacher would pee on the floor when he gets excited?

She Followed The Rules But To No Avail

Dear Dr. Gottlieb:

How do you do it—find the strength to go on each day? I always read your column and would listen to your radio show if I could find it. I know that life has dealt you some devastating blows. I wonder if you have deeper resources than I—possibly more faith.

There's hardly ever a day that I don't think of finding a way out, though it's important to make it look like an accident. The family shouldn't have to suffer because I can't figure it out. The kids are raised, the husband talks to me about 20 minutes a week, I volunteered, and have been on a hundred committees, baked and talked and marched for causes. I did what I thought I was "supposed" to do, and there doesn't seem to be anywhere to go from here.

What do you make of it?

Looking for the Checkout Line

Dear Looking:

I read your letter two or three times before I could begin to collect my thoughts and emotions. I felt frightened, sad, helpless, and angry. Angry because I felt so helpless and angry because I fight too hard for my life to let you give up on yours without my having a chance to understand you better.

I discussed your letter with several colleagues. They all had the same initial reaction—the same furrowed brow and confused look. Many had ideas and recommendations; but, mostly, they were concerned. I, too, am concerned.

Why does a letter like yours activate so much concern and energy? Poet Franklin Abbott said, "As a flower is drawn to the sun, it is the entropy of the human spirit to seek wholeness." Human instinct is to pursue life regardless of the costs. Your letter goes against our instincts. My drive to live my life despite adversity reveals only humanity—not heroism. What happened in your life that threw off your instinct to pursue wholeness? What happens in anybody's life that can cause so much pain that death feels like an improvement?

Your letter arrived several days after my column on loneliness. You described your loss of your children and husband and your attempts to cope with that loss. Any loss causes pain. The depth and severity of the pain depend on the intensity of the loss. After my accident 15 years ago, I was taken to Jefferson Hospital and I said, "Get me out of pain or kill me!" I was referring to the emotional pain more than physical. I didn't really want to die; I wanted understanding and relief. I think what most of us ultimately want when we are in pain is understanding. I was fortunate to have family, friends, and a therapist who were courageous enough to listen to my painful story without giving me advice.

When we are attacked by a loss, it is important to take stock of what it is that is lost. For example, when I became disabled, I lost my youth and my health. I lost my dreams for the future. These things were torn from my grasp. I was hurt, scared, and angry.

I would guess from your letter that among other things, you lost a dream; perhaps the kind of family you always wished for. I've seen many women dealing with issues similar to yours, and they are furious! They also lost their dreams. Many of them felt duped by their families, especially their mothers. They say things like, "My mother told me if I was good and caring, if I took good care of my husband and children, I'd be happy. I've done all these things, and I'm not happy. I've lived my life according to rules that don't work."

Sufi Indians say, "When the heart weeps for what is lost, the soul rejoices for what it's found." The date of your letter disarmed me—

December 20 is the anniversary of my accident. Thinking of that makes me miss the man I was and the life I had. I shed many tears as I mourned those losses. But today, I cherish my life like never before. What I found in the aftermath of my grief was life itself. Sure, I'd rather be walking; but if I was, I doubt that I could feel as deeply or have the wisdom I do today.

Before you look for a checkout line, let's understand what has been torn from your grasp, and what it means to you. I'd like to understand what you're feeling; the pain, outrage, or sadness—and, I am sure, I'm not the only one who would like to understand you better.

I would also like to suggest that you are not the only one in your family in pain, although you may be the only one who can feel or express it. It's been known for years that many women carry the feelings of their families. I wonder if your husband and children also feel a sense of loss but don't know how to express it.

It is also important to know that if you are vulnerable, any of these losses can trigger a major depression. The depression itself can contribute to your sense of hopelessness and futility. It can interfere with your ability to see options for yourself and can cloud your judgment.

With advances in medical and psychological treatment, depression can be relieved.

Every day we open a new door; behind it there are a variety of options—including a checkout line. If we pay attention, we can find a new adventure, a new crisis, a new way of coping with adversity, and possibly some sunshine and serenity. I hope when you open the door tomorrow, you will decide to call me or someone else who cares about you enough to explore all of your options before you look for the checkout line.

Faith And Belief

Dan,

I would very much like to hear your thoughts about people's belief in G-d as an aftermath of the recent school shootings.

It is very interesting how so many people search for solace in the religious community. It seems, when there are no answers, people turn to "G-d."

As you may have read, there is a movement to make Cassie Bernall (one of the victims in the Columbine shootings) into a martyr. She is the young girl who was asked by the killer, "Do you believe in G-d?" When she answered "Yes", he killed her.

Admittedly, I am an atheist. But my immediate question is, with her belief in G-d, why didn't her G-d save her?? Why, in fact, did he "allow" the shootings and killings to happen in the first place?

I am also confused and quite angry when parents remark that their child is "now with G-d". Or that G-d had another purpose for their child. It may be of some comfort for them to believe that since there really is no other feasible answer; there is no "Why".

The religious movement is growing fast and furious all around us. In my community, I see church after church building expansions to an extent that is unbelievable. TV evangelists are having a field day. Churches are using this tragedy for their own purposes and, at the same time, are exclaiming that they don't want to take advantage of the unfortunate situation.

A Reader

Dear Reader,

I am not a theologian, so I can't answer many of your questions about G-d's will or people's perceptions of G-d. But, as a mental health professional, I can talk about what helps the healing process when one has been traumatized. Research shows that one of the critical elements in both healing and resilience is faith. But, like a patient once said: "Does that mean I have to believe in G-d?" No, I said, "But you have to believe in something outside of your own will."

Some of the healing elements in faith are the ability to trust and give up control of that which we can't control. For example, when people experience crises like the parents who lost children in the Columbine shootings, there is no way a logical mind can comprehend this. Faith allows the logical mind to give up control.

On the other hand, there are many who believe in G-d but lack faith because they don't give up control. For example, when I was in my 20s, my wife was diagnosed with cancer that required surgery. Of course, I was terribly frightened. So, when they wheeled her to the operating room, I prayed.

My prayer went something like this: "Dear G-d, please take care of Sandy and this is how I want you to do it...!" Belief, but no faith.

Faith is about believing that if we do the right thing in life; be generous of spirit, contribute to community, show compassion for fellow beings—we will find more happiness and contentment. Having faith in a higher power doesn't necessarily have to be a belief that someone or something is "out there" and omnipotent. It also doesn't have to be a belief in heaven or hell. It can simply mean having faith in a piece of wisdom that lies deep inside your heart/soul and that you may never see it; but if you have faith, it will guide you.

Many of your questions begin with the word "Why" that suggests that you, like most of us, search for logic and explanation. Faith requires trust without logic or explanation. If we were somehow able to find a logical answer to our questions about G-d or how the universe is organized, that would deprive us of the opportunity for faith. Faith requires mystery.

Now, none of this addresses your major concern about abuse in the name of G-d or religion. Although most research addresses the benefits of faith, we all know that too much faith, or blind faith, can be dangerous. In the name of religion or G-d's will, people can rationalize anything including mass murder.

Ideally, one could look at mental health as the integration of head (thoughts), heart (feelings), and soul (spirituality). Faith without thought can be quite harmful and destructive. For example, most people who belong to cults have blind faith. On the other hand, relying too much on logic can leave one feeling empty at times of crisis.

I asked someone we'll call "Bev," a recovering alcoholic, how she understands her faith: "Sometimes, I believe in things just to make myself more comfortable. It is me alone who has to live with my sadness, my grief, my fear, and my guilt. Believing that G-d or someone is taking care of the results of my life (maybe not the daily operation, but certainly the outcome) is comforting. I have faith that will let me sleep more comfortably, act more wisely, and perform with less fear in my job and my relationships. Is someone watching all of this? Probably not. But my beliefs that I am cared for and that my loved ones are cared for are comforting TO ME."

Readers React To Faith Issues

I recently wrote about the role of faith in promoting mental health and well being. The column was written in response to a reader who was concerned about some of the reaction to the shootings at Columbine High School. He reported that he was confused and angry when people said that their children were "now with G-d."

In the column, I addressed the relationship between faith and well being, suggesting that faith required mystery and that too much factual information could actually interfere with faith. I also suggested that one could have faith independent of religious dogma.

Here's a sample of the reaction:

Dear Dr Gottlieb,

Greetings. Your column regarding faith piqued my interest, and I would like to respond.

Spiritual faith is of great interest to me; I consider it to be one of the world's silliest follies and those who traffic in it the worst of criminals and con men. It fascinates me how otherwise intelligent people have faith in something unseen, unproven, and objectively unknowable.

Now, to your piece. You make several statements which I assume you want to be held as factual that you simply cannot prove. When a patient asks if the belief in G-d is necessary for healing, you tell the person "No, but you have to believe in something outside of your own will."

Why? Who? What? Does one have to "believe" in the medical doctor? No, he/she is real. His training and experience or lack thereof is real. Belief is irrelevant. If not a belief in G-d, then a belief in what? What is superior to any human being that one can submit to for care and healing? Next you say faith "allows the logical mind to give up control." In other words, faith is an "illogical" process.

A Reader

Dear Dr. Dan,

I am not a theologian either, but I am someone who has suffered, and my healing is now being assisted by my faith in G-d. I was a victim of domestic abuse from my husband for 19 years. When I made the difficult and dangerous decision to take my son and leave him, for the first time in my life I put my faith and trust in G-d that he would protect my son and I from my husband's threats to kill us if we left.

When I related the story of my life with my husband, a story of mental, physical and sexual abuse, my therapist was amazed at my resilience that saw me through. G-d has no control over the evil people will do. And true believers do not use "G-d's will" to rationalize the occurrence of mass murder. People in my church don't turn to G-d for answers; we turn to G-d for strength, guidance and comfort. G-d did not "allow" the killings. They were not committed with his sanction or by his inattention. For those of us who believe, we can find comfort knowing that someone we love has died and now resides in G-d's heaven even while we mourn their loss and their departure from us.

Signed,
A survivor

Dear Dr. Gottlieb,

When I read your column on faith, I was pleasantly surprised by your statement that one need not believe in G-d to have faith. That doesn't seem to be the message we're getting from most corners of our society. Like your other letter writer, I too am an atheist who finds our culture awash in a sea of spirituality.

I will admit that I could possibly use a little more "faith" as I have trouble seeing the positive side of things. But is non-religious faith enough? For many people, it does not seem to be. Could you write another column touching on this a little further?

Kenneth

From a mental-health perspective, faith is akin to the basic trust an infant requires in order to develop into a healthy adult. That infant must have "faith" that he will be cared for. Infants, who have this trust, tend to grow up with a greater sense of security and well being. Those without an environment that fosters trust are at risk for growing up with anxiety and insecurity.

There is a growing body of scientific evidence that suggests those with faith are happier. That could mean faith in a higher power, faith in the benevolence of the universe, or faith in the goodness of their fellow humans. Frequently, matters of faith and spirituality are deeply personal and private. True faith, like the trust of the infant, frequently evolves from within; and the ritual and dogma of religion can either enhance or destroy that faith.

Most religions do invite us to be kind, compassionate, and of generous spirit towards those who have less than we do. In following those particular guides, the dogma can have a positive impact. There is even a recent discovery that endorphins are released and increased happiness is fostered by helping others. However, the ritual of religion can have a negative effect on someone's faith if a personal belief or desire is "unacceptable" by their religion. Positive or negative, faith can be impacted by religion; but it certainly exists independent of religion.

And to Kenneth—is faith illogical? Perhaps, but I see people in my office almost every day who are frustrated because their sense of logic failed to help them solve their problems. Sometimes a solution to a problem involves letting it go and having faith that it will work out on its own.

Purpose, Not Possessions, Brings Happiness

It was Susan's first session, and she was angry with her husband of 25 years. She blamed her depression and loneliness on his emotional withdrawal and hectic work schedule. "If only my husband was capable of intimacy, showing his feelings and being open about them, then I'd be more contented; then, I'd be happy," she said.

Richard was 37 years old and unhappy with his life. He had thought he would be more successful by this time. He was working hard at a job that wasn't very secure. He was sure he would be less stressed and his marriage would be better if only he made more money.

Both of these people, and many others like them, reminded me of my childhood. I never felt I was as good as the rest of the kids; not as smart or athletic. When I got my first job as a psychologist, I told myself that, if I worked hard enough, I would eventually have enough authority and prestige so that I would finally feel good enough. Four years later, I was working two jobs and had begun to gain the respect of my professional community. I also had early symptoms of a spastic colon. My work never quite got me there. Despite my successes, I considered myself good but not good enough.

It seems we're all busier than we want to be; rushing through the day to manage our lives. Time off means catching up on unfinished work or helping the children with their lives. Ever wonder what everybody is really looking for? The answer's simple: security and happiness.

To paraphrase essayist Wallace Stegner: We get possessing and belonging confused. The real wish is to belong; we try to possess more and more things and tell ourselves we belong to the things. Problem is, it doesn't work. People who have acquired wealth and material goods are no happier, or even more secure, than the rest of us.

According to a study headed by Eunkook Suh, of the University of Illinois at Urbana, external events have little or no influence on a person's well-being and long-term satisfaction. In a controlled study, they discovered that external life events—even major ones such as a marriage, winning a lottery, or the death of a loved one—didn't affect people's overall sense of well-being. The effects of external events tend not to last more than three months.

If hard work, changing a partner's behavior, or more money won't help us find happiness, what will? This is where family values come in, not the political, but the deeply personal kind that most of us don't think about.

In preparing for a talk I recently gave to the associates of a large corporation, I asked many of them to tell me about their jobs. I wanted to know about the ratio of work to pleasure, how many hours they worked, and how they felt about their lives in general. I learned that their average work-week varied from 55 to 70 hours. Most said that although there was some enjoyment, much of the week was devoted to stressful hard work. My last question in the interview was always the same: "Why do you work so hard?" Almost everyone would pause a couple of seconds. Then, the answers came: "money," "security," "making a name for myself." The answers were different, but that pause was always there.

Two seconds of silence. In that short span, the people I interviewed took a first step toward reflecting on their lives. I routinely ask my patients what they feel their lives are about. I ask what they want to accomplish between now and the time their lives are over. I rarely get an answer.

Our busy schedule is part of the reason we tend not to reflect on our lives. But, if we had a better understanding of our deeply personal values and purpose, we just might find that our lives are more manageable. We've been hearing a lot of talk about family values, but there are no family values without personal ones.

I recently met with a couple from North Philadelphia who were both working full time and raising five children; and they were able to answer the difficult questions. They said that their lives were devoted to protecting their children from the drugs, violence, and poverty in their neighborhood. They said that if they accomplish some of those goals with most or all of their children, their lives will have had a great deal of meaning. Despite how hard they worked and how little they played, they both were happy with their lives.

A friend of mine spent a year working with a volunteer organization in Africa. When he got back, he said; "This was one of the hardest years of my life, but the most instructive. I learned that for me to be happy, I need to give something back to the larger community." Psychiatrist Victor Frankl attributed his ability to survive the Nazi concentration camps to his understanding that his life had purpose. In his case, the purpose was to write a book about human existence that became one of the most popular books of all time, *Man's Search for Meaning*.

We are happier if we have an understanding of the purpose of our lives and live accordingly. When the gap between who we are at our core and what we do with our lives gets too wide, something inside begins to die. Family values are not about what we say; they are about how we live.

Summoning the Forces to Heal After Injury

It seems that nearly every letter I receive is about some kind of an injury. Every caller to my radio program and every patient I see also speak about injury. I hear things such as "My husband had an affair," or "My child is disabled," or "I was abused," or "I lost my job," or "I just found out I have cancer." These are the voices of the injured; we've all been there—after all, it's part of being human. Some of us visit this land of the injured more often than others. Some of us get stuck there. To cope with their injuries, some cry or scream; some seek retribution; and others seek the refuge of illness; loved ones, or psychotherapy.

Why do some get maimed by an injury, while others survive, and yet others seem to take it in and flourish?

How can we reclaim what we lost when we were injured and move on? Must we understand what was wounded before we can begin to heal?

To explore some of these questions, I talked to Mary Lou Schack, co-founder of the Gestalt Therapy Institute, who is set to share the keynote speaker duties with me at a conference called "Through Injury to Healing." I asked Schack what all of these different kinds of injuries have in common. She pointed out that "psychological injuries, like physical injuries, cause wounding and take something away from us. These injuries may take away our happiness, sense of safety or trust in people, and sometimes they take away our youth."

"We are often left with a sense of loss, terror, anxiety, or abandonment. These are typical legacies of significant psychological injuries. Even in ideal conditions, when healing is possible, we are left with scars that cannot, and perhaps should not, be forgotten. If we do forget, we are at risk of leaving a piece of ourselves along with the memory."

I asked her to describe some of the ingredients necessary for healing to take place. She explained that with the exception of loss, almost all psychological injuries take place in connection with others. Therefore, for healing to be effective, it should also take place in connection with another person.

"Some call these people 'healers,' but that's not accurate," she said. "They really provide a context for healing because healing comes from within. A real healer is more like a midwife for the journey. What we need from this person is what I call the Six H's of healing."

1. **Holding.** When we are injured, we need to be held in our pain. This may or may not involve physical touch, but we must be with someone who can tolerate our pain. Too often, people try to talk us out of it because they're uncomfortable.

2. **Hearing.** The person has to have the courage to hear and try to understand our injury and what we are going through.

3. **Heart.** This simply means the person conveys a message of caring and love.

4. **Humility.** This person realizes he or she cannot fix us, only support us.

5. **Humor.** If needed, he or she can provide a lightening of our burden through humor.

6. **Hope.** He or she can help us believe that we will heal.

Despite Schack's observations about the elements of healing, I've known many injured people who have had many of these ingredients and were still "stuck" and unable to move on. I've also seen people, who only had one or two of the H's available and not only survived, but grew and embraced life as well. What's the difference between those two types of people?

I believe that part of the answer can be found in genetics. Some people are just born with different levels of resilience. Other factors that affect how people cope with injury include emotional, social, economic, and family resources. Although I agree with Schack that healing takes place from within, I've discovered that having outside support and nurturing sure helps.

Perhaps most important is to understand and embrace the person who was injured. In 1979 I had a disabling accident that broke my neck and left me permanently paralyzed. Who was I before the accident? Who was I afterward? I didn't know. I was in agony. Reassurances that I would "be okay" were no comfort. Relief came only when people had the courage to sit with me as I struggled to voice my confusion and figure out what of me had died and who I was now.

We all encounter losses or traumatic injury in our lives. It is human nature to fight change and loss, but injury changes us whether we want it to or not. The problem is that we desperately try to hold on to who we once were. "After all," we say, "it isn't that bad," or "I'm okay anyway."

When we hold on to the old myth of who we were, we can never become who we really are; older, wiser, and scarred.

It's frightening to have our identity changed against our will. It's frightening to leave what we were comfortable with and go on to the unknown. To the best of my knowledge, there's only one way to begin this journey. Perhaps it's best described in a poem called "Daydreams." It was anonymously written by a person who knows something about leaving the comfortable place of old pain.

Come to the edge.
We might fall.
Come to the edge.

It's too high!
Come to the edge.
and they came
and he pushed
and they flew.

The Problem With Hope, It Can Hinder Recovery

Dear Dr. Gottlieb:

My brother-in-law has a mysterious illness, which caused him to lose the use of his hands and feet. He is 40 years old and is perfectly well otherwise. He is a professional and practices out of his home. He has had a lot therapy, and with the use of modified tableware, can eat by himself.

The problem is he almost never leaves his house. He sits in a manual wheelchair that he is unable to use independently. He has never explored motorized wheelchairs or modified vehicles. Every time I talk to my sister about taking advantage of the technology available to the handicapped, she gets angry and says, "Don't give up hope. Nobody can live without hope. I still believe he will recover."

Because they still have hope, they have not made any changes in their lifestyle. It has been over five years now and still no recovery. I always thought hope was a good thing; now I'm not sure.

Concerned and Confused

Dear Concerned and Confused:

Hope is one of the most frequent causes of depression. Of course, what I really mean is unrealistic hope. Many people I see are depressed, angry, or frustrated because they've been trying for too many years to accomplish something that can't be accomplished. Their energy devoted to this effort interferes substantially with their ability to enjoy their lives. Some spend a lifetime unsuccessfully dieting, but they still have hope. Others stay in a miserable job or marriage hoping.

As a quadriplegic, I've often felt that hope can be a curse. In a strange way, I'm lucky. I've known exactly what I had to look forward to since the beginning of my disability. The doctors were honest enough to tell me that, at this point, there was virtually no hope that I would ever walk again. When people tell me there is promising research in spinal-cord injury, I smile and say, "Keep me posted" while I resist the seduction of hope. Hope can drain one's energy and interfere with the normal and healthy process of mourning losses. In short, this kind of hope could diminish the quality of life.

Many years ago I saw Woody Allen doing stand-up comedy. He opened his monologue by saying, "I was breast-fed on a falsie!" I've thought about Woody Allen and that line many times over the years. My fantasy is that if I ever met him, I would say, "Woody, no matter what you do, no matter how much therapy you have or how much fame you achieve, it will always be a falsie! Stop being a victim of your history. Give up hope." So, you see, hope can be a curse.

On the other hand, hope can be a blessing. Your sister is right. We can't live without it. My daughter, Alison, who is now 21 years old, suffered from migraine headaches since she was 10. She would get as many as two a week during periods of stress or anxiety. When she didn't have a headache, she lived in fear of them. Over the years, she grew more irritable. I took her to many doctors without success.

This last summer, however, I sent her to a program that specializes in the evaluation and treatment of headaches at Germantown Hospital. After a seven-hour examination, the doctor gave her capsules that she was to take daily in the morning. He said they should diminish the frequency of her headaches to about one a month. He also gave her an injectable medication that, he said, should diminish the intensity when she did get a headache. That afternoon she behaved like a different person. The wrinkle that had been etched in her forehead for the last 10 years was suddenly gone. She was smiling and warm and seemed genuinely happy. And she hadn't taken her first pill yet!

When she left the doctor's office, the only thing that was different was now she had hope. Hope for a future relatively free of pain. Hope for a future that was free of fear of recurrent headaches. Hope for a future that could be hers and not one dominated by these demons.

We're still left with your question: Is hoping a good thing or a bad thing? The answer is both. Last month I was working with a couple who had been married nearly 30 years. Both partners had been unhappy with each other for most of those years. In this particular session, the wife was complaining about her husband's lack of involvement in the house. "He just comes home and reads the paper," she complained. "He doesn't seem terribly interested in my life and my feelings."

She had been complaining about this for more than 15 years! All this time and work with no success, but she still had hope. After spending much of the session clearing out the verbal debris, she finally realized what she was doing. At the end of the session, she put her head in her hands and said, "I feel hopeless about him."

That statement opened the door for some real change in her life. Now that she was ready to stop fighting this futile battle, she was less dependent on her husband for her happiness. A couple of weeks later, she told me that she thought for a long time about leaving the marriage if this was to be her future.

Eventually she decided that even though he wasn't the ideal husband, she was going to stay with him anyway. She said that she was initially grief-stricken after the decision, "Almost as though something I had been carrying for many years had died. At first it was terrible, sad, and painful; but at the same time, it felt like a relief."

Her loss of hope gave her the power to reclaim her life and stop waiting for her husband to change. It gave her hope for the future. We all need hope for a decent and pleasurable future. If the day comes that your sister and brother-in-law stop waiting and hoping, they can begin to grieve their losses and go on to rebuild their lives; I hope so anyway.

How A Serious Injury Damages The Body And Soul

Dear Dr. Gottlieb:

I need to know how to pick up the pieces of my life following an injury in a car accident. I'm injured seriously enough to be in constant pain and unable to work without tears, but not seriously disabled. It is difficult to make long-term plans when your physical abilities vary daily, monthly, yearly, etc. Please discuss how to deal with a traumatic event and its repercussions.

Carol

Dear Carol,

I don't pretend to have the wisdom of Job; but, unfortunately, I too was in an automobile accident. Mine took place 12 years ago and left me a quadriplegic. Traumas like the ones we have experienced have a significant impact on body and soul.

Part of what makes pain worse, and this applies to any kind of pain, is the feeling of isolation we experience. We live in a world where near perfection is perceived as the ideal and anything less is shameful. We feel, for example, that we must be the right weight, strength, and income bracket. When we are not, our imperfections become a source of shame.

Nothing creates a sense of isolation more powerfully than when we are embarrassed about who we are or what we feel. When I first had my accident, I hated myself (read "Shame") because I was not who I thought I should be.

In addition, most of us "learned" in our families that to feel pain is to be weak. We heard things like, "Be strong; don't give in to it." So, not only do you feel the physical pain, but you may also feel weak and not entitled to the support you need.

Carol, please understand that your body has been assaulted by an automobile accident over which you had no control. As a result, you suffer unavoidable pain. You are entitled to your fears, anger, sadness, and resentment; there is nothing to be ashamed of. Hiding or withholding your pain can make it worse.

Fortunately, there is much work being done on pain management in this region. Many rehabilitation hospitals have programs designed to help people in chronic pain. I spoke with Clarinda "Coco" Margolis, of Margolis Associates, a well-respected pain program in Philadelphia. She suggests that a comprehensive pain program has available neurologists, psychologists, physical therapists, and psychiatrists who can address the many different aspects of pain. Some treatment options include relaxation exercises, biofeedback, medication, and group and family therapy.

The impact of this type of trauma on the soul is difficult to wrestle with. There is a Sufi saying I'm fond of, "When the heart weeps for what is lost, the soul rejoices for what is found."

Carol, you lost more than a healthy body. We all have expectations of our lives and our futures; these are the most significant losses. I lost Dan Gottlieb as I had known him for 33 years. I had to mourn the death of a future in which I would play golf and racquetball and be powerful and graceful. I also lost the trust that I would be safe in a benevolent world.

I shed many tears over these losses. When I was ready, I found the truth in that Sufi saying. I gained the opportunity to be comfortable being a vulnerable man and be free of a good deal of the shame I had always carried. Therefore, I gained a greater access to intimacy with more people, and I gained the wisdom that comes from being disenfranchised.

We have known for many centuries the ingredients required for healing both body and soul: time, air, sunshine, and water. Please be generous and tolerant enough to allow time for healing. Give your wounds plenty of air; don't hide them from others. When you are ready, share your injury with people who care—that provides both air and sunshine. Water represents the nurturing from both the people who love us and ourselves.

I am learning to live with my paralysis and pain and navigate this beautiful and fragile life. I wish the same for you.

The Valuable Lessons A Patient Teaches A Therapist

After I finished a session with a patient the other day, I looked at the calendar and realized that as of this month, I've been practicing psychology for 25 years. After a quarter of a century, I think it's time to reflect on some of the things I learned and how I've learned them. One of my most important lessons is that what I have learned from my patients and my life experience dwarfs what I've learned from my professors and journals. I still read the literature and go to lectures, but I listen to my patients very, very carefully.

My first "real" job was in May 1969 at Mercy Douglas Hospital in West Philadelphia. The ink was still wet on my graduate degree, my head was swimming with information, and my heart was filled with insecurity.

I remember my first psychotherapy patient. Norma was a 65 year-old woman with schizophrenia. She shuffled into my office, heavily medicated, with several sheets of paper in her hand. I was so nervous; all I could do was look at the clock and count the minutes. I had no idea what was involved in this business called psychotherapy. I knew all of the theories, but this was a real person with real problems.

I didn't want to ask her why she was tearing these papers, as I didn't want to upset her. I knew if she got upset that it would be a bad session. At the end of our time together, I breathed a sigh of relief and told Norma she could leave. She shuffled to the door, stopped, and slowly turned around. She looked me in the eye as she laughed and said, "You know something? I think you're full of crap." She held up her torn papers and hollered, "And I've got the papers to prove it." Norma was right. And I was desperately trying to hide it. Norma and I went on to have a wonderful relationship after I acknowledged to myself that she was not my patient—she was my teacher. She taught me that a real healer cannot lie and cannot hide. A wounded soul always knows when there's a lie in the room.

Throughout my practice, my patients have been my teachers. They have taught me about their pain, and the courage it takes to face that pain. They have taught me about their creativity and integrity in navigating their way through some very stormy waters. They've taught me most about the value of listening, bearing witness, and how true understanding dignifies someone's experience.

I've learned that when someone says, "You don't understand," they're right. I've learned through their life experiences and mine, the courage it takes to truly trust another human being. Whether that relationship is marriage, partnership, or psychotherapy, trust is terrifying.

About six months ago, a woman named Caroline called to ask if I would see her. She recently had had surgery for colorectal cancer and was told that it had metastasized. In our first session she asked me to help her with issues of assertiveness, self-esteem, and setting boundaries. I agreed to help her with these issues if she would agree to help me understand more about life and death. I have realized that the more I am able to face death, the more I am able to appreciate my life. She looked at me quizzically when I invited her to be my teacher but agreed to do so.

As her cancer got worse and her complexion grew grayer, her anxiety-related symptoms seemed to dissipate. We reflected over her life and pending death. As we talked, I watched as her terror turned to fear and the fear turned to anxiety, and the anxiety turned to unhappiness. As her eyes grew darker, her wisdom grew deeper.

Caroline invited her daughter, Natasha, to come to a session with us to talk about unfinished issues in their relationship. I watched with awe and admiration as this now elegant, graceful, and courageous woman helped her daughter cope with her mother's impending death. She wept for her daughter's loss. They embraced and said goodbye to each other. I was struck by what a privilege it was to be present at a moment like that.

Last week Natasha called to say the end was very near. She held the phone to my dear friend's ear as we talked for the final time. We talked about whether she felt ready for this moment we had talked about for six months. I needed to know if she was at peace. We acknowledged that we loved with each other and said goodbye.

I will be forever grateful at how well Caroline did the job of teaching me about life and death. It's one of many lessons I have learned over these 25 years. I've learned that many things don't change. Such things as our history doesn't change, nor does the scar tissue left from our wounds, and it's especially important to know that our loved ones rarely change.

When we find a way to live with these truths, life becomes richer. I've also learned that knowledge comes from books and wisdom comes from experience—both my personal experience and my experience with my patients. Many of my most important lessons have come at times and places I've least expected. Yesterday someone called to make an appointment to see me. I can't wait to meet my next teacher.

Hope Cuts Both Ways

I was watching the recent Super Bowl with several friends. Everybody was pretty relaxed, sitting either on the sofa or floor; except me. I sat where I always sit—in my wheelchair. Like most, we were talking during the commercials when, out of the corner of my eye, I saw a fellow quadriplegic—Christopher Reeve. All conversation stopped as we watched him rise from his wheelchair, walk haltingly across the stage, and accept an award. Conversation seemed to stop and, all of a sudden, I felt terribly conspicuous—and terribly crippled. I felt exposed, embarrassed, and enraged. This was a commercial for John Nuveen & Co., an asset management firm that spent 4 million dollars to deliver the message, that people could "change the way they think about wealth." Boy, if only people could change the way they think about one another, what to do with one's wealth would be less of a problem.

Hope cuts both ways.

It's been 20 years since the automobile accident that left me paralyzed; and in that time as a family therapist, I have treated more than 100 people with spinal cord injuries. Depending on their emotional and social resources, most do quite well. Many get depressed for a period of time but most recover. Of course, their lives change. Many marriages don't survive, and some people are forced to change careers. But, for better or worse, life goes on for most. But not for everyone. I have treated many people who were more crippled by hope than by the spinal cord injury. These people don't reclaim their lives. They stay home and wait for the cure. I have watched as they sacrificed their time, their families and, for all intents and purposes, their lives—waiting for tomorrow's cure.

Hope cuts both ways.

Several months ago, when I interviewed Reeve for my radio show on WHYY, he referred to himself as "temporarily quadriplegic." When I told him that I had very mixed feelings about the idea of cure, I explained that I had spent 20 years living my life in a chair and that I was pretty happy. He said that my position was understandable because of the life I had made for myself. I attribute part of the quality of my life to hopelessness! I was told there was no hope for a cure, and I believed it. So, after a period of severe depression, I began looking for a way to find happiness in a wheelchair. I never had hope that I could walk, but I always had hope that I would be happy.

Don't get me wrong; hope is also necessary for life. Poverty without hope is lethal. Hope is a critical element with cancer and many other diseases. But even with cancer, hope cuts both ways. When diagnosed with a serious illness, hope gives us energy to fight the necessary battles and helps give us a vision for a future without illness. Hope can stave off an incipient depression. But I have also treated many who were terminally ill and watched as hope turned into denial and robbed them of quality in their final days. How sad it is when someone is near death and their loved one says, "Don't give of hope," instead of saying, "I love you dearly and will miss you forever."

So why was I angry? Many in our society become objectified. Not just those of us with physical or mental handicaps but often racial and ethnic minorities, women, children and senior citizens are seen as "things"—as faceless members of some group. When that happens, we become a little less human. Life-sustaining compassion stops, and we are told who we are by others.

The Nuveen commercial tried to tell the world what we wanted and how we would look if we got it. Well, if the people who made it were to come to me, I would tell them what I really want. I would want them to look at me as a man and not a thing. I would want them to make eye contact with me and learn about my humanity—things I love and fear. The daily suffering of quadriplegia and the daily joys of being alive—even in a wheelchair! I would ask for their caring instead of spending 4 million dollars to manipulate people to invest with their company. Later, I read that some people with spinal-cord injuries thought at first that Reeve must have been cured. But they weren't the only ones who felt harmed.

Personally, hope scares me to death. I built my life, I like my life, and I see talk of a cure on the horizon as an expectation that my life could change radically again. I wouldn't say no, but I sure wouldn't be the first one in line. I'd get there when I get a break in my schedule.

The gift of a cure involves diminishing some suffering. The price of a cure is a radical change in this life that I love. I'm no different from you. My psyche is the same as yours. You suffer with a whole variety of things, and you incorporate them into your life. How about if I gave you a million dollars and tell you as a result of that you might not be seen by your community, your friends, and even your loved ones the same way as you were yesterday? Wouldn't you think twice?

I also feel people would be less compassionate toward me. I get to see the best of humanity in how people behave toward me. I see these kids at the mall looking tough and acting threatening; but when they see me, they stop and say hello. I fear I might lose some of the many, many things I've gained as a result of my spinal cord injury; the wisdom, the ability to sit still and observe, and my own ability to slow down and feel compassion.

When I first saw the commercial, I felt so ashamed and vulnerable. If the people responsible for the commercial felt those emotions, I would have more hope. But I don't.

The Readers Respond

I recently wrote an article about a Super Bowl commercial sponsored by John Nuveen & Co., an asset management firm. The commercial centered on a computer simulation of quadriplegic Christopher Reeve walking. In the article, I talked about my sense of shock, exposure, and outrage when I saw the commercial. I explained how hope cuts both ways and that sometimes hope can save a life, and sometimes hope can destroy one. For example, there are many people with spinal cord injuries who refuse to live their lives because they are waiting for a cure. Likewise, I have seen couples battle terminal illness; and because of "hope," they never get to say goodbye to one another. I was also angered by the assumption that all people in wheelchairs just want to walk. I suggested that people in wheelchairs want what everybody else wants—to be understood and ultimately to be happy.

I am a Hospice Nurse and have been a nurse for twenty-four years. I too had the same reaction as you did when I saw this commercial. I felt so angry with the Nuveen Corporation for not showing compassion to all of my precious, courageous patients who hated to be told that they could control their lives if they "invested" the right way. I wept for all of us. The image was so disturbing to me. Hope scares me, too. I cringe when someone makes a declaration of hope for a cure or a "war on…" this or that disease.

And, yes, it would be so much nicer if at the end of life, all the people involved would just say, "I don't know what to say to you. All I know is that my heart is breaking, and I am going to miss you".

Is Life this mystery, or is it quite simple?

I only want to mention that I saw the ad during the Super Bowl, but being a wife and cook, I tune out most TV advertisements as I prepare for dinner. I did catch that one though and felt it grotesque to say the least. I had no idea of the sponsor but felt subliminally that someone was taking cruel advantage of Mr. Reeve. Please G-d, some day we'll advance enough to find a "cure" for these terrible injuries; but as of now, we seem a long way off. I know we all need hope—but hope mixed with a sense of reality.

I don't know how to thank you for that column. As a pastor for 37 years, I cannot comprehend your experience, making it through what you did, but, I would see it as G-d working in you to bring healing—and I know we both understand the many shades and dynamics of healing.

I know you are well beyond having difficulty sharing your feelings—but I thank you for the view inside…

I just wanted to applaud you for your article in *The Philadelphia Inquirer* on Feb. 7. I was actually appalled by the Christopher Reeve commercial during the Super Bowl. I thought it was in very poor taste. It is wonderful that he is able to use his celebrity to raise money, but I feel that that commercial may tend to give others a false sense of hope.

I was touched by your story in last Monday's *Inquirer*. I found the commercial of Christopher Reeve walking in very poor taste. I found it very disturbing. I am glad you wrote about it and let us know what it was like to encounter it from your position.

I too had seen the spot and felt very uncomfortable about it but couldn't articulate the feeling until I read your article. Wow! This led me to the realization that recently I have been feeling nostalgic about the year I had chemotherapy for breast cancer. While it was a fear-filled time that I would never want to repeat, I was the recipient of so much love and support and came away from it with a new and deeper capacity for joy-in-the-moment. If the cancer returns, all bets are off; but for now, I'm not sure I would erase the experience if I could. I think you understand what I mean.

My son was injured 11 years ago in a hockey accident. This article so reflects his feelings, and it was refreshing to read. Like you, he also will not be the first in line (if a cure comes). He lives his life teaching 6th graders and continuing his education. Would we like this to be different; or does it make me sad? Of course it does. I saw a perfectly healthy 18 year-old college freshman turn to dependence again; but the gifts he brings to each day, not only to his family but the other people he touches, is certainly an unexpected gift.

Thanks again. These words are what spinal cord-injured people need. This is what gives us all something to hold onto—remembering that these people have wonderful contributions to make to this world.

I had not fully realized just how the messages Reeve puts out could be harmful. Fortunately, I guess, I have not had to devote a lot of thought to it. But it was so helpful to read from a different perspective and to realize the implications of a driven focus on getting people out of wheelchairs and on their feet. You helped me to see all that is implied in that. Your words will help us to focus more clearly on deeper values and on seeing people and treating people as people; not as something or someone who could be better off. There are many kinds of crippling. Thank you for sharing your perspective and helping me examine my attitudes.

You expressed some of my sentiments about the Chris Reeve story. Isn't it ironic that we only grow from adversity? I can especially relate (in your article) to the denial my husband and I both showed toward the end of his life. In our hearts we knew the end was near, but neither communicated this to each other, but why didn't I say something? This I have yet to come to terms with.

I don't remember my immediate reaction to the Christopher Reeve commercial on Super Bowl evening; but on reflection, it was thought provoking and maybe troubling. Yours however was an interesting perspective that I hadn't considered. Happiness is ultimately what life is all about. If you have been able to achieve happiness while having accepted the fact that you are likely unable to walk again, that is the best scenario for you. If Christopher Reeve's quest to perhaps walk again one day provides him with happiness, that is the best scenario for him.

Congratulations! Someone finally spoke out about that terrible commercial!!! Because we are also part of the disability community, I shared your sentiments and feelings. We were stunned; as were so many others to whom I have spoken. It was cruel and tasteless.

Life's Too Short To "Own"—Just Being And Belonging Are The Keys

I was in Florida last week for a brief vacation and a visit with my parents. During the week, my father and I spent some time at the ocean; talking, watching, and just being. I looked at his face, and he looked more relaxed than usual. This is an experience I, too, commonly have when I'm near the ocean. I turned to him and said, "Dad, I think if I could watch the ocean for an hour a day, I'd live a longer life."

Several hours later I was taking a "walk" with my friend, Roberta, and reported the story to her—how I'd like to watch the ocean for an hour a day. After several moments of silence, I turned to her, half jokingly, and proclaimed, "I've made up my mind; when we go home from vacation I'm going to work extra hard, make lots of money, and buy the ocean and take it home so I can watch it whenever I want!"

Sadly, it was only a half-joke. Sad because I think it reflects much of the mentality I see in today's world; that is—if you like it, if it's good—then try to own it.

The essayist Wallace Stegner once wrote, "We get belonging and owning confused; our hunger is to belong—in order to deal with that hunger we try to possess."

We live in a country where three out of 5 people move every five years. That means very few of us have the sense of belonging that our parents and grandparents may have had. The need to belong is a very human one. Look at some of the examples of our hunger to belong; clubs, organizations, 12-step programs, membership in inner-city gangs, synagogues and churches—all reflect, among other, things that we need. So we try to possess things to feel connected and more in control.

But if we can look back over our experiences, we will discover that when we try to own things that shouldn't be owned, they die a little bit. This includes our environment, children, spouses, and even our bodies.

Last month I had a consultation with a young woman who was recently diagnosed with a chronic illness. She was depressed, not by the illness, but by her inability to control her body. With a frightened look she complained, "I'm exercising; I'm watching my diet; I'm surrounding myself with good people—and yet I still feel weak. I feel guilty that I'm doing something wrong, and I'm angry with myself. If only I could figure out what I'm doing wrong, I would fix it; I'll do anything."

I asked her to describe the experience of being ill, and she was unable to answer. She had no experience looking inside and describing what it was like to be who she was. She was far more experienced at looking outside and controlling something; calories, appearances, whatever. As a result of her power struggle with her body, the very thing that will keep her alive now becomes an enemy—not unlike what happens in many marriages.

How does she work out her relationship with her body (really her soul)? Perhaps just by being, listening, and not controlling—doing some of the same things my father and I did when we watched the ocean. After all, who watches the ocean and tries to control the waves! All you can do when you're at the ocean is just be; how healing that is. We need to do that with our environs, our bodies, and our loved ones. Much of Chinese philosophy suggests that our soul is really an empty vessel filled with temporary things. Our children, parents, spouses, youth, health, and wealth are all examples of temporary things. If we try to "own" any of them, we will fail.

My brief Florida trip occurred a little over a year after the death of Darrell Sifford; *The Inquirer* columnist who was my good friend. He had always longed to be near the ocean for an extended period of time. He finally did it, and he died while that experience was in process. For those of us who knew and loved him, we owe it to his legacy not to forget his lesson.

About the Author

Psychologist / family therapist Daniel H. Gottlieb hosts the widely acclaimed public radio show "Voices in the Family." For 8 years he has authored a bimonthly column in *The Philadelphia Inquirer*, "On Healing." He responds to readers with advice from science, philosophy, poetry and his experience as a grandfather, father, son, brother and quadriplegic.

For information about submitting manuscripts for the People with Disabilities Press, please write: Stanley D. Klein, Ph.D. People with Disabilities Press P. O. Box 470715 Brookline, MA 02445

Printed in the United States
56670LVS00004B/26

9 780595 174836